Sex Without Sight

Sex Without Sight

and Other Stories

By Bob Bobala

Exit Strategy Press

"So Much Trouble With Animals" first appeared in *North Dakota Quarterly* (vol. 7, no. 3, Summer 2004).

"You Should See This" first appeared in *The Portland Review* (vol. 41, no. 3, Spring 1995).

ISBN 978-0-6151-8025-0

Exit Strategy Press

To my Mom and to Nick Allocca.
I'm all for exit strategies, but I wish you'd waited a bit longer.

CONTENTS

Sex Without Sight

and Other Stories

So Much Trouble With Animals

The monkey was on the attack. Again. Geraldine knew this because she'd seen that her gas grill had been overturned and her petunias shredded.

As soon as she got home from her shift at the bakery, she called her house to order. Her children, Emma, Clive, and Samantha, marched into the living room.

"The monkey is loose," she said. "I'm sure of it. You know the drill: all doors, all windows locked. After I inspect Clive's room, you'll go there, and stay there until I say it's okay to come out."

Clive, the middle child at twelve, protested. "I don't want the baby in my room," he complained. "I don't want her messin' my stuff."

Geraldine gave him the look that she often gave him on these weekends when she was tired of all of them, tired of working 3:00 a.m. to 11:00 a.m. with the smell of cheese Danish making her nauseous, tired of them acting up because she'd banned chocolate donuts from the house because she couldn't stand the sight of them.

She had the same *look* the other day when she smashed a stale French baguette over Clive's backside after she'd found crumpled pornographic magazines stashed underneath his bed. "You want to know more about sex?" she'd said. "I'll show you more about sex!" After hitting his body, the bread snapped in two and half of it flew across the kitchen. She sent him to his room and buried the magazines in the trash. Later, she felt her reaction had been too harsh and that sooner or later she'd have to speak with her son about matters that were important.

While the children were asleep she pulled the magazines out of the garbage and flipped through one of them. There were close-up photographs of a man with dirty fingernails touching a woman's private parts. The pictures made her feel like vomiting—not only because of their vulgarity, but because they reminded her of the last man she'd been with. He had been an auto mechanic whose hands were permanently stained with oil and grease. After she complained to him, he would sit in bed with a file and pick at the dirt underneath his fingernails, flicking black specks on the carpet. Whenever he touched her with his sandpaper hands it was all she could endure. When they made love she would get on top and pin his wrists down so he couldn't touch her anymore. For Geraldine, it was an act of self-defense, but to this man it was erotic. "I never had no woman take charge of me like you do," the man had said. This went on for three months, until she took the job at the bakery and told him she could not sleep with him any longer because she would be working nights.

Now, with the monkey on the loose, Geraldine resisted the temptation to whack Clive up the backside for acting up. She simply took a step toward him and gave him *the look* one more time. It was a look she was conscious of, one she had perfected in recent years—the look of fury, exasperation and crazed danger, with one eye cocked and the other squinting, staring down upon her subject with an incredulous inquiry into its very soul. The weight of it bore down on Clive and he took a step backwards.

"Your sister is not a baby anymore, and we have a situation here. I need your cooperation. You're the man of the house."

Like a soldier reluctantly receiving orders but nonetheless committed to carrying them out, Clive did an about-face and led the other two children toward his room. Samantha, seven years old, held the hand of the oldest, Emma. As they passed by her, Emma kissed Geraldine on the cheek and wished her luck, as if Geraldine were departing for battle and her daughter didn't know if she would ever see her mother again. "I'll take care of Samantha, mom. Don't worry," she said.

Geraldine had no doubt, which worried her enough. For the better part of a year, her eldest daughter had spared no sacrifice, sharing a room with the youngest, rising at nearly dawn and seeing the other two children off to school. Every day Geraldine was stunned by her maturity and mothering tendencies. The girl seemed to rise to every challenge. She slept with a stuffed moose at the foot of her bed and a baseball bat and canister of mace by the night stand. Geraldine was reasonably confident in her children's safety, since she didn't leave the house until almost 3:00 a.m. and Emma rose at 6:00 a.m. Still, she had a burglar alarm installed when her credit card limit was extended, and she bought a phone for every room in the house. She taped the numbers for her work, the direct lines for the police, fire, and hospital, as well as the digits *911* in big block letters on top of each phone.

Before her children entered Clive's room, Geraldine stopped them at the doorway and checked the closet and underneath the bed to make sure the room was secure. Then, she shut them in, telling them they could watch television as long they watched what Samantha wanted.

Leaving them, she proceeded to fortify the rest of the house. She knew exactly what to do. This had happened before.

The neighbor across the street had a monkey. Geraldine didn't know what kind of monkey, but it wasn't a good monkey like an orangutan or a chimpanzee. It was some ugly, brown monkey with whiskers coming off its chin and a bare butt that it dragged up and down the sidewalk when it went on these rampages.

This monkey had been involved in some medical experiments, and apparently the owner gave it a home as if it were a stray dog. But this wasn't a house pet. This was a monkey, and it was wild and vicious. Geraldine, for the life of her, couldn't understand why the owner was so fond of it. All it did was fart, tear up flowers, and harass the neighbors when it got loose.

She'd had two other run-ins with the monkey in the past few months. The first time she'd caught the beast in her driveway, perched atop Samantha's Big Wheel, looking down on her and squawking like a bird. The girl just sat there on the asphalt, pointing up at the animal saying, "Hel-loooo, monkey." Geraldine reached for her broom, tore out of the house, and clocked the monkey straight across the jaw. It rolled across her front lawn, screeching wildly, then ran across the street where it dragged its butt up and down the sidewalk. This went on until the owner came out of his house and coddled the monkey in his arms. The monkey slapped him in the face and tried to break free, but the owner held on and brought it inside. All this, Geraldine saw from her living room window, Samantha clinging to her leg.

Her second brush with the monkey was even more disturbing. One of her potted plants had been knocked over on the back patio and she spent considerable energy reprimanding the kids, none of whom would claim responsibility. And then she was folding clothes in her bedroom when she heard scratching coming from her closet. It sounded as if her shoes were being tossed about, and as she approached the door she heard a squawk and the monkey bounded out of the closet, leapt up at her chest, ripped her glasses off her face, and darted out of the room. The children ran about the house screaming as the monkey went from the bedroom to the kitchen to the living room in a wild frenzy. Clive threw a baseball at it and broke a lamp. Samantha, the most valiant on this day, brought out a slingshot and launched marbles at the monkey as it scuttled back and forth on the coffee table. She missed each time, and since then had taken to calling herself Sammy, and sometimes Sampson, because she said if she were a boy she would have struck that monkey dead right there in the living room.

Finally, Jared came over to find out what was happening and the monkey bolted out the opened door, the kids chasing after it, screaming, "Die like a pig, you stinkin' monkey" and "Stay outta our turf or we'll break your neck."

Geraldine was appalled that her children would use such violent language and embarrassed because they'd used it in front of Jared. She had no idea what it meant to die like a pig, and Clive using the term *turf* alarmed her and she'd watched him closely since then to see if he had been hanging with his gang friends again.

If there was a silver lining to any of this, it was that Jared, her next door neighbor, had come over to see if they were okay on both of the previous monkey attacks.

"Gerry, is Samantha all right?" he'd said through the living room screen the time the monkey had co-opted the Big Wheel. He was the only person who called her *Gerry*. She didn't even know why or how he started doing that, but she liked it. It created a certain kind of intimacy with him that she shared with no one else. She was mortified the last time he came over, after the monkey had been in the closet. The monkey had scratched her across her chest, ripping her shirt, and she wasn't wearing a bra. Jared had brought her children to her mother's, and then brought Geraldine to the hospital, insisting she get a tetanus shot. And as the doctor steadied her breast with one hand and sterilized the wound with the other, she imagined he was Jared for a minute, and she liked the way his clean hands felt.

The tetanus shot punctured her fantasy rather quickly. It was the second one she had gotten in three years, the last one coming after a stray cat she was trying to befriend bit her on the ankle in her front yard. As they walked away from the hospital, Jared's arm draped over her shoulder, she kept mumbling to herself, "Mama keeps telling me that I have so much trouble with animals. So much trouble with animals."

Her mother kept telling her a lot of things, most of which

Geraldine tried to ignore. "All those animals that keep bitin' you, those bees that keep stingin' you, they got spirits inside. They tellin' you somethin'. I don't know what, but they tellin' you somethin'. You gotta find out, girl."

Her mother was the most superstitious person she knew. She walked around with a salt shaker in her purse and every so often she would throw a handful of salt over her shoulder. Geraldine had no idea what this ritual was about, but she surmised it warded off whatever evil spirits were around at the time. Whenever she'd catch her in the act, her mother would just give her a sheepish, girl-like smile, her false teeth sticking out of the top of her mouth. "Every little bit helps," she'd say, and she'd even sprinkle salt on Geraldine's doorstep as she was leaving.

The last time the kids stayed at her mother's place, Clive had a stomachache and her mother put sliced onions underneath the bed while he slept "to draw the poison out of him." He came home the next day saying, "I don't want to go back to Granny's. It stinks!" Geraldine's mother was quick to point out, of course, that by morning he was cured and ate three stacks of her flapjacks.

Her mother buried broken pieces of a mirror in the backyard to avoid bad luck. She saved her fingernail clippings and burned them every year on New Year's Day. She would sing to the netherworld as if she were living in it on a daily basis. As a child, Geraldine remembered sitting in her mother's lap in a rocking chair, asking her mother who she was talking to. "No one," she'd say. "They're not people. You don't know them. You might someday." Then she'd go on, humming and singing, "Spirits, keep away from me. I gotta keep shinin' on…. Evil spirits, keep away from me. I gotta keep shinin' on….."

The songs piled up in Geraldine's mind over the years and she even found herself singing some of them occasionally, especially since she'd been working at the bakery. The rhythms and the sounds made the time pass more quickly, even if she didn't believe in any of the words or understand them.

Her mother, for her part, only seemed to get worse with age. The latest was that she was trying to improve Geraldine's love life. "Three children and you're getting up in your years. You need a man," she said. "A good man, though, not one of the ones you normally give yourself over to." Apparently the solution to this was lettuce. "It has the power to arouse love," her mother said. Twice a week her mother would come by with a head of lettuce—iceberg, romaine, green leaf, red leaf, she'd tried it all. "You're not eating enough salad, child. That's your problem."

She'd met Jared a couple of times. After they were done at the hospital on the night the monkey attacked Geraldine, he brought her to her mother's house to pick up the kids. Her mother looked him over closely. She walked by him and sniffed by his right side—much to Geraldine's chagrin. Later, in private, she said to Geraldine, "I can't tell about him. Spirits weren't talkin' when he was in the room."

After the second monkey attack, Jared also had helped Geraldine get restitution for her glasses, which they found in three pieces on another neighbor's hibachi. They were expensive glasses, more expensive than any pair she had ever owned. But she allowed herself at least one nice thing a year, and these glasses had framed her face beautifully. They made her look years younger, she thought. The man who owned the monkey refused to pay for them at first, but then Jared went over there and said he'd break the monkey's neck himself if Geraldine didn't get reimbursed. Still, they no longer made those frames, and Geraldine had to settle for a pair of glasses that made her look her age. And she saved the broken, useless ones because she had a secret plan. One day she would move to a better house, with a fireplace and a mantel over the it, and she would have those old, beautiful glasses mounted on a stand, encased in Plexiglass, and she'd keep them up there on the mantel to remind her of how good she used to look, and to have a monkey story to tell each time her grandchildren came over.

Jared also helped her take action to have the monkey put to sleep. He told her all the people to call, and even called the city himself. Geraldine was adamant about the monkey's destruction. "It attacked me and my children!" she told one official. "The monkey is a menace."

But it was useless. She was told that the city pound, which would have jurisdiction in this case, no longer had the money or the staff to carry out such an operation.

"Then maybe we should carry it out ourselves," Jared had said, and that was the last thing he had said to her, over a month ago.

During the first couple of weeks she didn't hear from him, she imagined he was secluded in his house, trying to come up with a plan to take out the monkey—a plan they could carry out together. After that, she figured he just wasn't thinking about her, but she didn't know what he was doing. He had been divorced, too, with one child. But she never saw any other women coming out of his house. She found it strange that their whole acquaintance revolved around the monkey, but she'd take what she could get. She picked up the phone and called him. His machine answered and she started leaving a message: "The monkey's loose again, and I need your help."

She immediately was frustrated for making herself sound like such a victim in need of rescue. She was about to hang up when he came on the phone.

"Geraldine? That you?" he said.

This was not a good sign. He was no longer calling her Gerry. He *must* have another woman over there, she thought. Why else would he be so distant? He said he would come right over, but it seemed to take him quite some time, particularly since they were in the middle of such a crisis. She was beginning to question whether or not she could still depend on him.

Finally, he came over with a baseball bat in one hand and a black trash bag in the other.

"I'm gonna knock that monkey to kingdom come," he said, breathing heavily, as if he had already been in a skirmish with it.

Geraldine went toward him, as if to hug him, or thank him for coming, or something. But before she could get close enough she heard Clive yelling from the kitchen.

"Whoop his ass, Jared! I'll be right behind you."

"What kind of language is that?" Geraldine shot back at her son. "Get back to your room. You're supposed to be protecting your sisters."

"You gon' bash his skull in, Jared? We gonna have monkey brains on the sidewalk?"

Geraldine gave her son *the look* again, and he went back to his bedroom, his voice trailing off, saying, "I'm for monkey brains on the sidewalk."

"I'm sorry," Jared said. "I didn't mean to stir things up."

"Oh, things are already stirred up around here. Don't worry about that." Then, without much of a pause, she said, "How are you? It's been so long since I've seen you."

But before he could answer, she got up and continued shutting the windows, feeling like a fool for trying to flirt with him given the gravity of the situation. The monkey was on the loose. This was no time to be thinking of how long it had been since she'd been with a man, or at least with a man she liked.

Geraldine and Jared canvassed the house to make sure the monkey wasn't already inside, locking doors and windows as they went, Jared leading the way with the bat, Geraldine following with the trash bag. Once she was confident the house was secure, she went into the kitchen and called her mother to ask if she could bring the children. "The monkey is loose again. I just want the kids outta here in case it gets ugly," she said. But what she was really thinking was that she had an opportunity to spend some time alone with Jared.

"You should be wearing an opal," her mother said to her. And then, "Is that man there?"

"Yes, mama."

"Well then, I'd sure love to see my grandchildren, wouldn't I?"

"No onions this time, mama."

"It's time for you to tend to your business, child."

Once she got off the phone, she called out to Jared, who sat watch in the living room. "Ma says the kids can sleep at her place tonight. I just have to bring them over."

"I'll do it, if you like," he called back to her.

"That'd be fine," she said. She liked how he wasn't afraid of her children, how he enjoyed them, even. During the time of the last incident he'd joked with Clive, carried Samantha in his arms, and held Emma by the hand as if they were his own.

Jared went next door and pulled the car around. Geraldine readied the children.

Clive protested. "I don't wanna go to grandma's. I want to see monkey brain get splattered."

The look silenced him.

Samantha carried her sling shot at the ready, fully loaded, with extra ammunition in her pockets. "But what if Mr. Monkey follows us to granny's?" she said.

"Now, I won't let that happen. Don't worry about that. You just go have fun at granny's," Geraldine said.

"But what if the monkey gets you?"

"The monkey's not going to get me, sweetie. I'll take care of the monkey."

She kissed her on the forehead as Jared honked the horn in the driveway. Geraldine stepped outside first, the baseball bat in hand. There was no sight of the monkey, and she started to wonder if all this was for nothing. She hadn't actually seen the monkey today; she'd just gone on a hunch, some destroyed flowers, and a tipped-over grill.

But as Jared began to pull away, it came out of the shrubs beside a neighbor's house, dashed across Geraldine's lawn, and leapt onto the hood of the car. It pressed its face up to the windshield and squawked at her children, who in turn screamed with all they had, Emma ducking down in the back seat, Clive shouting "Kill it! Kill it, mom!" and

8

Samantha with her sling shot aimed and ready to fire.

Geraldine clutched the bat and ran toward the car, but Jared honked the horn, then quickly backed out of the driveway and sped off down the street. The monkey rolled off the hood and ran to the sidewalk in front of a neighbor's house where it scraped its butt and then darted off into the backyard.

Geraldine stood in the warm breeze for a minute, watching to see if it would come back, then she went into her house to prepare for the next attack.

She did not know much about monkeys. But once, not too long ago, when she'd been struck with a fever and flu, she had watched a *National Geographic* program about a river that dried up in South Africa. Apparently, there had been a long drought—though this did not surprise her because she thought there was always a drought in Africa—and animals from all over had sought out this river in the middle of a desert. There was no current left in the river, though. It had dwindled to a shrinking, stagnant pool, surrounded by black mud. Birds, hippos, fancy deer, crocodiles, and monkeys were dependent upon this last source of water for survival. And with the exception of the hippos, the crocodiles threatened every animal that tried to drink from that pool. The crocs yanked more than one of those fancy deer down into the murky water and had themselves a feast before the water completely dried up and they all died. But what Geraldine remembered most distinctively was when one crocodile locked its jaws around one of the monkeys' heads. It was one of the most horrifying things she'd ever seen. At first the croc just lay still with the monkey trying wildly to get its face out from between its jaws. Then the croc seemed to grow bored with the monkey's struggle; it rolled over, snapping the monkey's neck, and then glided into the deeper end of the pool, the monkey carcass hovering above the water like a trophy until it submerged into the darkness.

The night she'd seen the program she became delusional as her fever worsened, and she dreamed she was floating on her bed with monkeys surrounding her, screeching at her as she tossed and turned, tangling herself in her blankets until she thought she might choke. At the end of the film, they had shown monkey and crocodile skeletons, drying up where the water used to be. In her feverish state, Geraldine could feel bones drifting all around her. At one point she picked them up and threw them at the monkeys, shouting: "It's not my fault. I had nothing to do with it!"

She swore she clobbered a couple of monkeys with those bones, but the rest of them just kept screaming and dancing, bouncing up and down, waiting for her to completely pass out so they could move in for the kill.

She had been an animal lover all her life, and in the past she had been bitten by dogs, stung by wasps, stepped on by a cow, kicked by a horse, and defecated on by a sheep. But she held no grudge against any of these animals. Even the cat that attacked her on her own front lawn had not caused her any great ill will toward animals. But somehow monkeys, and this one across the street in particular, were different. This one had to be terminated.

While Jared was away, she quickly straightened up the house. She cleared Samantha's toys out of the living room, ran a sponge over the coffee table, and washed the dishes that had been sitting in the sink. She wanted to take the trash out because she knew buried at the bottom of it were Clive's dirty magazines. It was risky to go outside alone, but she wanted the magazines out of the house, lest Jared or anyone else notice them. She feared the monkey was out there close by, plotting its next move. There was no doubt in her mind that the monkey was calculating. It did not randomly wreak havoc in the neighborhood. It was selective. She was sure of this like she was sure she'd bake exactly four lemon-meringue pies on Monday, and three of them would sell by Tuesday night and the last one would be fed to her boss' Dalmatian, who had a sweet tooth like no other animal she'd ever seen.

She thought about killing the monkey, wondering if, when the time came, she would be able to go through with it. Outside of ants and a stray fly or mosquito, she didn't recall ever killing anything in her life. Her brother had been the killer in the family. Even as a child, she remembered he was always experimenting with various kinds of animals. He used to staple frogs to wooden planks in the sun and burn out their eyeballs with a magnifying glass. He had exploded an M-80 under a cat. He used to throw stones at birds and once she saw him crush a possum's head with a cooler full of ice. He joined the army when he was eighteen, then blew himself up during an artillery drill somewhere in Nevada. At the funeral, his sergeant praised him for his initiative, saying, "I know T.J. was proud to die serving his country, and I'm proud of him. There isn't a man in our platoon who wouldn't have entrusted his life to him. His fightin' spirit will always be remembered."

That was over twenty-five years ago. Geraldine's mother was

despondent for months after the death. She had wanted more than two children, but her third was a miscarriage and the doctors had to remove her uterus. Finally, as she was coming out of her depression, she said to Geraldine, "We have to keep up our fightin' spirits. We have to fight on." Geraldine had always felt she failed in this respect. She had not fought to keep her husband when he was leaving her. She had not even fought for Clive last year when he was wrongly accused of shoplifting at the Safeway—she just paid the bill, vowed never to shop there again, and now drove ten minutes out of her way to buy groceries at the Giant. She questioned if she would have enough gumption to actually bring the bat down on the monkey's head if given the opportunity. She tried to imagine what it would sound like—if she could bear the crunch of the bone. She knew it was something she would have to do, though. Like trying to befriend a stray cat, or getting a tetanus shot, or sleeping with a man whose fingernails were never clean—you did what you had to and hoped for the best.

She grabbed the bat and swung it in the kitchen, accidentally knocking over her tea kettle and a box of week-old sugar cookies she'd taken from the bakery. It felt good, though. The bat was a far better weapon than the broom she used to knock the monkey off the Big Wheel. One quick pop with it and Mr. Monkey was history. "Gonna knock your block off, monkey," she whispered to herself. "Die like a pig."

The garbage had to go outside; she would take the risk. She threw the old cookies in the trash and peered out her back door window, ready for combat. The yard was quiet—too quiet for a Saturday afternoon, as if the whole neighborhood was on alert and her neighbors had all shut themselves up inside their homes, awaiting the outcome of this final battle with the monkey. There was no sound of lawnmowers, or hedge clippers, or cars running, or children yelling, or any of the other sounds she normally heard on the weekends when the weather was nice. Only the lazy trickle of a sprinkler swaying back and forth over a mound of crabgrass next door caught her attention.

She stepped outside. There was no sign of the monkey, so she felt like a terrified fool when it blind-sided her, jumping off the roof onto her back, clinging onto her sweater and squawking like a bird until she flung it off of her. She took a mighty swat at it with the bat, but missed its head by a good foot and it darted between her legs, ripped open the unprotected trash bag, dragged it across the lawn, and then retreated through the sprinkler in the yard next door. She eyed it as it scampered out of site, her heart pumping.

"Come on back, you coward monkey!" she shouted after it. "I'll be waiting for you! You and I have an appointment!" Then she muttered to herself, "I've got to be an idiot. I'll be damned if some monkey gets the better of me."

She pounded the bat into the ground, furious at herself for missing an opportunity to end the whole thing. She wouldn't be humiliated again. "That monkey's mine and mine alone," she mumbled to herself. It had become personal. That fightin' spirit welled up inside of her. Her cheeks felt like they were on fire. This was a sign that someone is talking about you behind your back, her mother had said to her once. She paused for a moment, wondering who could be thinking ill of her at the moment. There was a long list—her ex-husband; her ex-husband's second wife; the principal of Clive's school, who she called incompetent after he tried to put her son in remedial classes; her boss, who complained that her donuts were too fat and not "cost effective"; the paper boy, who'd held a grudge against her since she'd given him a quiche as a tip at Christmas time. They could all take a number, though. Today, there was just the monkey. "Tend to your business," her mother had said to her. And so she would. She gripped the bat tightly, thinking that everything would be different once she whacked this monkey. Outside of providing for the safety of her children, she didn't know why this would make such a difference in her life. But she had a feeling her cheese bread, and her blueberry turnovers, and her cinnamon twists would never be the same. From here on out she'd make the fattest donuts on the eastern seaboard if she wanted to. Nobody would stop her.

She got the barrel from the other end of the small yard and began gathering up the garbage that the monkey had strewn about. Among the refuse was a chicken carcass, freeze-pop wrappers, empty Pixie Sticks, and just what she wanted—Clive's porno magazines spread across her lawn. She thought that sort of thing was natural for men, but a twelve-year-old boy gawking at women who were twice his age, with breasts bigger than the size of his head? It was ludicrous. And she didn't understand the women who posed in these magazines, either. Many of them were beautiful, with beautiful bodies. Didn't they know how much power they had? Why did they waste it so quickly on men with dirty fingernails? Why did she do the same?

She flipped through the magazines and found a range of images. Some were repulsive, with sex acts between men and women, and women and women, and groups of men and women. Others were more glamorous, with beautiful women in glossy photos, looking like queens. She read some of their names. There was Marissa, who played tennis in the nude and liked to watch horror movies. Nelle, who spread her legs across a red car and liked hockey. Kobi, who was only 5' 1" and liked to cook wearing only her teddy.

There seemed to be two kinds of women in the photographs. There were these queens, and then there were the others, the ones who were probed by ugly men who hadn't shaved, with big bellies and balding heads. Many of these other women were contorted in various positions and they looked like they were in pain. It was a stark contrast to the queens, who lay on nice beds with satin sheets and fluffy pillows. They wore silky lingerie and high heels. They held their butts in the air and smiled, or they had a seductive look on their face, or they looked like they were turned on, anxiously awaiting a man. They wore make-up and fancy hairstyles. They looked pampered. Their pictures were glossy and airbrushed so that none of their flaws would be revealed. They looked like goddesses.

She wondered how her life would have been different if she looked like any of the women in these pictorials with their long legs and thick lips and fake boobs. She wondered if her first husband would have still run off with a skinny, white woman he met at the greyhound track. He lived with her in New Orleans now. Every time she pictured them, though, they were sitting there sipping drinks, betting on dogs as they ran around and around, chasing a fake rabbit, or was it a fake monkey? Geraldine couldn't think of a sillier thing. But picturing them that way helped ease the pain of his betrayal. "Go off and waste your life," she had said to him. "Just don't ever come near my children again."

Sitting there on her little back lawn, with the magazines on her lap, she wondered what it was like to have thousands of men looking at your picture. Did it take away all your privacy? Did men look at you differently when they saw you on the street or in the grocery store? Did they know? Did they know that when you weren't looking for bargains in the meat aisle that you were a goddess?

Back in the house, Geraldine washed her hands and face in the kitchen sink and then went into the bedroom to change. She took her clothes off and stood in front of the mirror, looking at her body. She removed her glasses and put in her contacts. She poked at the bags underneath her eyes and stuck her tongue out as if she were at the doctor's office. She cupped her breasts. They were not sagging badly— at least, she didn't think they were. She never considered them her strongest feature, but she still noticed men in the post office with their eyes fixed on them. Her skin felt tight and dry and she rubbed lotion on her arms and legs. Years ago, her husband used to say she had the softest skin he'd ever felt. She wondered if that included the greyhound chippie he ran away with. She hoped she still had something over her. She dabbed perfume on the back of her neck. She put on her best pair of jeans, a tight T-shirt with no bra, and a pair of sandals that she'd worn only once before. She rinsed her mouth out with mouthwash, put on a subtle shade of lipstick, and was ready to go.

She found a bottle of Beaujolais on top of the refrigerator, tucked away behind a package of egg noodles and a box of Cream of Wheat. She dusted it off and put it on the kitchen countertop with two glasses. The wine was a leftover gift from last Christmas. She could not remember who had given it to her. She did not drink alcohol much, and when she did it was usually beer. When she worked normal hours, she used to occasionally take some satisfaction in coming home after work in the evening, putting on her slippers and privately drinking a can of Budweiser or Schlitz, or whatever her ex-husband might have in the refrigerator. But it didn't make sense to have a beer when she got home from work now, at eleven o'clock in the morning. Once the monkey was taken care of, she would ask Jared if he would like to celebrate with a bottle of Beaujolais. This, she was sure, would make her sound much more sophisticated than offering him a Bud.

"The kids are safe," Jared said as he got out of the car.

Geraldine met him in the driveway, the bat clenched in her hand. She surveyed the roof of her house and the television antenna. "He's planning another attack," she said. "He's calculating and conniving. He came after me in the backyard while you were gone. Jumped off the roof and got me by surprise."

"Are you okay?" he said, hugging her gently. She wrapped one arm around him, keeping the bat by her side with her free hand.

"I'm fine," she said. "I had a clear shot at him, but I missed. I won't next time."

He let her go and surveyed the area. The street was still quiet. "Let's go inside and decide what to do," he said. "We're sitting ducks out here."

Jared reached for the bat as they went up the steps into the house, but Geraldine switched the hand she held it in and squeezed it until her knuckles turned white. He held the door open for her and touched her shoulder as they entered the living room, saying, "We'll take care of everything."

Inside, they paced around the living room, trying to come up with a plan. "We've only got a couple hours of daylight left," Jared said. "It'll be harder to find him at night." He was of the opinion that they should hunt the monkey down. But Geraldine said they couldn't go into the neighbor's yard. She wanted to take him out while he was trespassing on her property——that way if the neighbor called the police she could prove her actions were in self-defense. She pictured several squad cars coming to the scene, like a homicide, with police personnel standing over the monkey carcass, one of them outlining the body in chalk. They'd question her and write down what she said in their little notebooks. "First it was my petunias, then it was my grill, then it was my children," she'd say. The monkey threatened my whole family. It was self-defense!"

Jared didn't want to just passively wait for the animal to attack again. "We should trap it," he said. "We should lure it." But the best plan they could come up with was to put bananas on the front lawn, wait for it in the bushes, and then surprise it. The whole prospect of it sounded ridiculous to Geraldine, like something Samantha had said to her when the monkey had gone on its first rampage last year. "Mommy, if you want Mr. Monkey to like you, leave some bananas for it." Geraldine smiled at her and patted her on the head, saying, "I don't think this monkey likes anybody."

They decided to be patient and let the monkey make the next move. Geraldine made some iced tea and brought it into the living room, where they established an outlook by the big window where they could see past the front yard into the street. They made small talk and Geraldine caught him looking at her breasts more than once. She offered him a piece of old cherry pie she'd brought home two days ago, but he declined politely.

She admired his temperance. He was in good shape for a man in his forties, unlike her ex-husband, who had been overweight. She could only imagine how big he would have gotten had she been working at the bakery and bringing food home when he was still around. Even so, the greyhound woman he ran off with couldn't have weighed much more than 100 pounds. Geraldine had seen her once. When her ex-husband came to get some of his things, she sat in the driver's seat of the car, the engine still running. Geraldine stepped out into the front yard and beseeched her to get out of the car. "Come on out," she said. "I just want to see what you look like, that's all. I want to see if you're the garbage hauler who's gonna take my piece-of-trash husband to the dump."

A slinky, white girl with long, curly hair stepped out of the car. She had to be in her mid-twenties. "Honey, you're gonna need help," Geraldine said.

Then, as her husband came out of the house with his arms full of clothes, she clocked him straight across the nose. "You're gonna ruin this poor girl's life, too?" she said.

"Get back in the car, Marguerite!" her husband said, blood dripping on his white shirts. "I told you to stay in the car!" They sped away with the girl clutching the steering wheel and him holding a pair of boxer shorts to his nose.

She was about to ask Jared how long he had been married, but at the last second kept her question to herself. She didn't really need to know anything more about him. He'd given her family support when they needed it; that was enough. She liked just sitting quietly with him, not asking him anything more about himself and not having to divulge anything more about herself.

They sipped the iced tea and Geraldine wondered if it would be inappropriate to put on soft music and sit a little closer to him. It didn't seem right. It was still daylight, and it was warm. Even with the fan blowing, she could feel sweat beading up on her forehead. There was a monkey on the loose, but the children were gone and there was silence. She did not have many opportunities like this.

She ran her fingers up and down the smooth neck of the bat, feeling confident that she could take the monkey out with one swing if she had another chance. "Die like a pig, you monkey" kept reverberating in her head and she cursed her son silently for ever uttering the phrase.

He asked her questions about her children and about parenting, and she answered them thoughtfully, glad she didn't have to say much about herself. He smiled warmly at her when he made eye contact, when he wasn't looking out the window. She giggled at the funny things he said about his own son, who lived with his mother and her new husband in California. She touched his hand occasionally.

Once during their conversation the monkey came out and dragged its butt up and down the sidewalk across the street, but then it darted behind his owner's house. Jared tensed, but Geraldine caressed his arm, saying, "As soon as it gets in our zone."

She went into the kitchen to get him more iced tea. When she came back, she was dismayed to find he now held the baseball bat between his knees. She held his glass out to the hand that held the bat, hoping he would let go, but he took the iced tea with his free hand.

As the sun began to fade, she realized how hungry she felt for the first time. "Why don't I make us something to eat," she said. She fried two catfish fillets that had been sitting in the refrigerator. She took out a loaf of pumpernickel that she had baked two days ago, but before she could slice it she heard her mother admonishing her in her head, saying it was bad luck to slice a new loaf of bread without making the sign of the cross on it first.

Geraldine thought the prospect of this was ridiculous, but she found herself running her finger over the bread in the shape of a cross anyway—anything to avoid bad luck this evening. They sat down to dinner in front of the living room window. He ate quickly and quietly, soaking up the grease with the two-day-old pumpernickel. It occurred to her that she hadn't seen a man eat since the auto mechanic, who belched and chewed with his mouth open. Jared ate compactly, almost daintily, wiping his mouth after every bite. "It was delicious," he said after cleaning his plate. "I didn't realize how hungry I was."

They sat quietly for a minute after he finished eating, then Geraldine lit a candle on the coffee table and brought the Beaujolais from the kitchen, the glasses clanking against the bottle. "I was saving this for after the deed was done, but I think we could use a drink now."

He smiled awkwardly and said he'd have a glass or two to relax. It'd been a long work week. Now the monkey had taken over the weekend. He said he didn't regret it, though. "At least it's given me the opportunity to spend some time with you, Gerry. It's been a while." He smiled, held his glass up in a toast and then kissed her on the cheek. "Thank you for dinner and for the wine."

Buoyed by the kiss and the fact that he called her Gerry again, Geraldine leaned in to kiss him on the lips, but then they heard wild scampering across the roof. They both stared up at the ceiling as the noise crisscrossed the length of the house. They followed it into the kitchen and then to the back door where the monkey scratched its feet against the screen while hanging from a gutter. Jared flung open the door and monkey screeched at him, then dropped to the ground and bolted, Jared in pursuit, bat in hand. Geraldine grabbed the broom and tore out the front door to try to head it off before it could get back to its home base. "He's mine!" she shouted, but the monkey was too fast for both of them. It flew across the street and disappeared into a patch of bushes. Jared hacked at the shrubs with the bat while Geraldine screamed for him to stop. "It's gone! It's not here," she said, feeling guilty that she was actually relieved the monkey had escaped.

Back inside the house, Jared was agitated. "It's dark already," he said. "We're too vulnerable at night. We should have hunted it down earlier."

He paced back and forth in the living room, the bat resting on his shoulder. He cupped his hands against the window and tried to look outside. "You can't see anything unless it's under the street light. We're sitting ducks in here." He pressed his face against the glass and sighed, the moisture from his breath sticking to the window. Then he was back to pacing with the bat on his shoulder.

"We're safe in here," Geraldine said. "Let's just regroup. We'll have another chance."

This was not going the way Geraldine had expected. The wine had barely been touched. She had not had a chance to play her soft music. She couldn't get Jared to sit back down on the couch with her. She was quickly losing control of the situation and she couldn't stand not being in control in her own home.

He excused himself and went to the bathroom down the hall, but even then he carried the bat with him. He shut the door and she heard him put the bat down finally. His departure gave Geraldine a minute to think, and the thoughts she had were radical. They made her giddy and she giggled for a second but then screwed up her face and got serious. She licked her lips and ran her fingers through her hair. The toilet flushed. He ran the faucet for a long while. Long enough for Geraldine to get completely undressed. When he came back, she was perched naked on the couch, up on her knees. Her back was arched, her clothes crumpled beneath her. Jared hovered over her in the candlelight, his shadow looming large on the wall. He dropped the bat and it knocked hard against the coffee table before rolling to a stop on the floor. He went to the window and closed the blinds tight.

*   *   *

Geraldine did not sleep well. It had not gone the way she planned. She had imagined she'd be on top, but he had thrown her over on her belly and pinned her arms behind her back. He smelled of perspiration and he grunted and made noises like an animal. He touched her in ways that hurt and he thought this aroused her. When he was done he tried to hold her and caress her gently, but she couldn't stand the feeling of his sweat all over her. Once he fell asleep she wrapped herself in a sheet and tried to sleep on the edge of the bed.

She kept imagining she heard the monkey, though, screeching from her neighbor's yard across the street. A couple of times she started, thinking she'd heard it on the roof again. When she finally did fall asleep she dreamt she was walking through a vast desert, searching for water. There was a pack of monkeys along her path. Many of them were mating. They screeched at each other. They bit each other and ripped pieces of each other's hair out. The females scratched and clawed at the males' heads before they were overcome. The males dragged the females in the sand, twisted them around, pressed their faces into the desert floor, and pinned them against rocks.

Geraldine walked past them as fast she could, but she was losing strength, starving and thirsty. She walked alone and in silence for a long time. In the distance she could see a watering hole with enough water to last her for a long while. A feeling of relief washed over her and she felt content, as if the hard journey she'd just been on had all been worth it. She started to cry and thanked God that she'd made it this far. But then the monkeys came back and sped by her, chirping at her as she tried to keep up. She grew more tired by the minute and before long she gave in, resolved that the monkeys would drink all the water before she arrived at the oasis and she would choke right there in the sand. She dragged herself on her hands and knees up a hill to get to her final destination, expecting the worst. Yet, when she made it to the water there was plenty left, and there was no sign of the monkeys. She waded into the water, dunked her head under, and started to drink. She gulped down the water until her stomach hurt, then closed her eyes and let herself float. The hole seemed to get bigger and bigger, and she sank into its depths with her eyes closed. The cool water revived her and she relaxed, falling deeper into the hole until she began to feel what she thought were pieces of broken shells gouging her. She pushed them away, but the deeper she went, the thicker the debris became. Finally, there was so much of it on all sides of her that she feared she wouldn't be able to get back up to the surface. Then she opened her eyes and saw that she was surrounded by bones—bones of the monkeys that had come before her and drank the water. There were skulls and fingers and feet, and parts of arms and legs. All the pieces closed in on her and she began to choke. She kicked and thrashed and tried to swim upward, but she was only pulled deeper into the hole, into darkness, where she couldn't see and her air was running out.

She awoke to hear Jared's heavy breathing. Then she tossed and turned for the rest of the night, twitching because she thought she felt bones brushing up against her in bed.

In the morning she woke up with a jump, gasping for air as if someone had struck her in the gut. There was a shriek in the front yard, and then a *thwap* and then another. She shot up in the bed. Jared was not beside her. The ceiling fan spun slowly overhead and she felt dizzy, as if she were going to vomit. "You son of a bitch," she said out loud. "Damn you!"

She grabbed her robe and stumbled down the hall to the front door, not noticing the smell of the coffee or the bacon and eggs that sat on the table. She didn't make it outside fast enough to see anything except the black trash bag that Jared slung over his shoulder and the spattering of blood on her driveway and car.

She sat down on her front steps and folded her arms over her legs, a breeze blowing against her feet. He was barefoot, wearing only his jeans, and he walked like he was trying to avoid stepping on broken glass or jagged rocks. He dropped the black bag to his side and the sun shone brightly on his deep brown skin. She could see finely sculpted muscles in his back, and his arms were tight and defined. He put the bag in the trunk of his car next door, then jogged back over to her.

"It's over," he said, squinting down at her, sweat beading up on his forehead.

"I know," she said.

"Sorry about the mess on the car," he said. "I think it will wash away with water, but if it doesn't I've got some mineral spirits that will take it right off."

He went into the house and came back with his shoes and shirt. "I'm gonna dump it in the river. I don't think anybody saw it happen. But if anybody questions you, just send them to me."

He kissed her on the forehead before he left, but then drove away staring straight at the road.

She cinched her robe tighter and then went to the kitchen and tossed the breakfast Jared had made into the trash. "I don't need your *mineral spirits*," she said, mocking his words. "I got enough spirits of my own." She filled a pail with water and dishwashing liquid and grabbed a scrub brush from underneath the sink. The water slugged over the edge of the bucket as she walked, leaving a trail through the living room on out the door, all the way to her car. She dropped the pail on her driveway and turned on the hose. The water quickly enveloped the small patches of blood on the blacktop, bubbling over it and then rolling down the driveway. She got down on her hands and knees and scrubbed at the blood. It had splattered up on the side of the car near the wheel and on the hubcap. She took the brush to that, too. Her robe soaked with water. Her head shook with the momentum of the scrub brush. She began to chant one of the nonsensical rhythms her mother used to sing to her. "Spirits, keep away from me. I gotta keep shinin' on. Wicked spirits, keep away from me. I gotta keep shinin' on."

The suds flowed down the driveway to the curb, where a puddle began to grow until it found its way into the street. Her arms became sore and she scraped her knees against the cement. She could feel the sun on the back of her neck and her head began to throb. "Whoa spirits... Whoa spirits." She scratched her fingernails over the blacktop and broke a nail. Her legs were getting numb and she feared that soon she would be too cramped to stand up, but she didn't stop until the soap had run out. By then the water had flowed all the way down the street to the sewer.

The hose was still running when her mother's old Buick rambled into the driveway. Geraldine's children leapt out of the car and she sat back against the tire she'd just cleaned, watching their sneakers splash through the water as they came running up to her.

"What are you doing, mom?! The street's flooding all the way down the block," Clive said, always worried about the family image. "Didja go crazy or something?"

Samantha took her shoes off and slapped her feet through the puddles in the driveway. Emma shut the hose off. Clive ran into the house. Geraldine's mother stood in front of her, her knee-highs drooping toward her ankles. She wore an old, paisley skirt and thick-soled brown shoes that were cut out near the insteps to relieve the pressure on her bunions. Her skin was darker than Geraldine's and she had raccoon-like circles beneath her eyes, which seemed to grow deeper and blacker with age.

She put her purse over her shoulder and shifted the wig on top of her head. It was the same frosted, gray wig she wore to church every Sunday, the same wig she first wore at Geraldine's father's funeral five years ago. "I am old and gray and there is no use hiding it anymore," she told Geraldine as they rode home from the cemetery. "My husband is dead and I am not a woman anymore."

"What are you then?" Geraldine had asked her.

"I just be," she said. "I just be."

Back then it only sounded like another one of the strange things her mother said, but right now to Geraldine it seemed like the finest and best thing anyone could ever say about herself.

Her mother looked as frail as ever, and she moved slowly and methodically, shifting her feet back and forth as she looked over the driveway and the street. Her bones looked like they might snap if she moved too briskly. She put her fingers in her mouth and adjusted her teeth.

"I brought some lettuce," she said, grabbing the tops of some green leaves that were stuffed in her purse. "But it seems to me from this scene here that you need more than salad."

"No, mama, I'm fine," Geraldine said.

"Well, then at least cover yourself up, girl. Lying out in the driveway half-naked and soaking is not going to get you the kinda man you want."

"I know, mama." She pulled the robe tight over her chest.

"You takin' care of your goblins yet, Geraldine?"

"No, mama, not yet."

"Well, you be tryin'," her mother said. "I know you be tryin', and I'm proud of you for that."

"Thanks, mama. I just be."

Her mother stood over her and smiled. To Geraldine, she looked like she was over a hundred years old, but when she smiled there was still a certain vibrancy in her eyes that made her look ageless. Geraldine hoped that in thirty or forty years her own daughters would see the same thing in her when she looked down upon them. It wasn't the most she could hope for, but it wasn't the least either, and thinking about it made her feel content.

Samantha jumped into Geraldine's lap and nuzzled herself up against her. "Where's Mr. Monkey, mommy?"

"I don't know, sweetie. Maybe he took a cruise. Maybe he won't be back."

Clive bounded out of the house with an old golf club he'd found down by the train tracks. He swung it wildly in the front yard. Emma came outside. She'd changed into shorts. She strolled down the driveway with her long, birdlike legs, picking up the bucket and the bottle of soap. Then she sat down beside Geraldine and Samantha.

"Let that monkey come back around here now," Clive said, golf club in hand. "Whack!" He came over to the rest of them and inspected the car. "Ma, you didn't even do a good job washing it," he said. He ran and turned the hose on again.

"Clive!" Geraldine's mother snapped, and then Geraldine saw it. Her mother's eye was cocked and *the look* bore down on Clive until he sat on the driveway with the rest of them at her mother's feet.

They all sat there quietly, leaning against each other, facing Geraldine's mother's sagging knee-highs. The sun shone down brightly and it was shaping up to be a very hot day. The cool water from the hose ran underneath them, though, and the kids patted their hands and slapped their feet in it in harmony. Geraldine could feel the rhythm; it wove through her like her mother's songs used to. She searched for words to sing, but nothing came to mind, so she just watched her mother throw salt into the water, and then watched the water snake its way down the driveway and past the curb, where it flowed freely in the street.

Appaloosas, Morgans,
a Few Arabians

Jane Salimas might have been able to handle a summer with the Pajacks camped out in the backyard if they hadn't ruined her view.

The view was one of the reasons she chose to rent the Pajacks' house in Amherst. From the back porch, she could look out at the foothills of the Berkshires, green with trees and more comforting than what she'd grown up with in Wyoming.

The Rockies intimidated her. As a child, she once visited Jackson Lake and spent the whole day in the car while her parents roamed around taking snapshots of the surrounding mountains. She tried to climb out of the back seat, but each time she opened the door she became unbearably dizzy. The mountains looked ominous, black and jagged; from a distance she couldn't see the trees on them. At the end of the day, her mother dragged her out of the car to watch the sunset and Jane just crouched, staring at the ground, her hands clasped over her ears.

"You're going to regret not seeing this," her father said. "And, after this behavior, we're never coming back."

"They're too loud," Jane said, closing her eyes. "These mountains are too loud."

A month later, even the photos were too noisy for her. Her father hung one of them in the living room. There would be times when she'd accidentally look at it during the middle of a conversation and her thoughts would be scrambled and she'd completely forget what she was talking about.

But the Berkshires were much quieter. And after her husband, Gil's, nervous breakdown, it was Jane who suggested they try Massachusetts as a summer respite, and it was Jane who drove up to Amherst on a weekend in April and stood on Irene and Merrill Pajack's back porch, looking out over the state university's abandoned horse farm that sat at the foot of their property, and out at the Holyoke Range in the distance.

It was Jane who said, "It's perfect. I'll send you the check next week."

And she reached out and shook Mr. Pajack's hand. And Mrs. Pajack, her Shetland sweater draped over her brown paisley dress, put her arm around her and said, "Wonderful, dear. Wonderful! You'll love it here. You'll absolutely love it. Won't she, Merrill?"

"Absolutely," he said. "You'll love it. We're going cross-country, you know. To Wyoming, then to visit my wife's brother in Las Vegas."

"Wyoming? I grew up in Cheyenne," Jane said. "You'll love it. The Rockies are incredible."

"We're all going to have wonderful summers," Mrs. Pajack said.

Jane smiled. Looking out at the mountains, she decided that this place would be far enough away from New York for Gil to put everything behind him, though she wasn't sure if he understood exactly what it was he had to put behind him.

In March, he'd come home from work three hours late, soaked from a heavy downpour and shaking from the cold. He stood at the front door, his arms crossed, his hair hanging in his face, ringing the doorbell, as if he didn't live there anymore. He'd lost his keys and his wallet somewhere, along with his coat. Worst of all, though, was the look on his face—as if he'd never seen her before.

He kept saying the car had broken down, but he either refused to tell her where it was, or couldn't remember. For a day, she even thought he might have been having an affair.

She had seen the news that night with the commuter rail shootings. But the idea of her husband being on the train never even crossed her mind until some policemen showed up at her door holding Gil's coat two days later.

"You'll have a wonderful time here," Mrs. Pajack was saying.

"Yes," Jane said.

But now, in July, she saw that prediction would not come true. Her eyes couldn't get beyond the Pajacks' pop-up camper in the middle of the backyard, its flaps extended on each side as if it would take off into flight were it not secured by bricks behind each wheel. On one side of the camper the Pajacks had strung up a clothesline, wrapping it around the trunk of an old elm tree. Jane had no idea where they washed the clothes that hung on the line, but every day there was an assortment of undergarments and T-shirts. On the other side of the camper, they had stretched a canopy over the picnic table, attaching it to another tree at the other end of the yard. They ate dinner there, then played cards until long after dark by the light of their kerosene lantern.

In front of the picnic table and out from underneath the shade of the trees, less than ten yards from the steps that led up onto the back porch, were two lawn chairs, held down by sand bags that kept them from ever blowing over. Mr. Pajack had positioned them so that he and his wife could sit facing the sun in the afternoon. Usually they wore long pants and long-sleeve shirts, but from time to time Mr. Pajack would take off his socks and roll his pants up to his knees, exposing his white, hairless calves and grabbing at the grass with his fat toes.

Two hibachis sat a few feet in front of the chairs. When the couples were still speaking to one another, Mrs. Pajack had said they were "his and hers hibachis," given to them for Christmas by their son who lived in Georgia now. It was practical, she said, because sometimes she wanted chicken and Merrill wanted hot dogs, and it was better to cook them separately. On their first day back, the Pajacks had even invited the Salimases to have dinner with them. Merrill had picked up two kielbasas that were on special. He charred them on the grill and Jane tried to pretend she liked it.

All Gil Salimas knew about the Pajacks was that they were a retired couple with plans to finance a trip cross-country by renting their three-bedroom Victorian house for the summer. He hadn't even spoken to them until he and Jane arrived in Amherst during the first week of June, and even then he only wished them a safe trip. The old man, however, went on for a while, drinking a cup of coffee, asking Jane questions about her home state and babbling about a dead army major he had an affinity for who'd lost his arm in the Civil War and then had a monument erected in his honor in southern Wyoming.

"You ever been to Green River, Miss Salima?" he said to Jane.

"No, but I think I've driven through it once or twice. I've heard of it."

"You ever been to the Powell memorial? Major John Wesley Powell? The first man to navigate the Colorado River through the Grand Canyon. He started right there in Wyoming on the Green River. There's a shrine built in his name right where the journey began. Right there in your home state, Miss Salima."

Gil was pretty sure Mr. Pajack was not doing it on purpose when he pronounced *Salimas* without the *s* or when he addressed his wife as if she were an unmarried woman, but he wasn't completely positive, and he felt uncomfortable renting a house from a man who might have been making fun of him every time he opened his mouth.

"The Major has always been one of Merrill's heroes," Mrs. Pajack cut in. "He's read his book about the struggle down the Colorado and Merrill says not once did the Major mention he had only one arm."

Only after she said that did Gil notice Mr. Pajack was not holding his coffee mug by the handle, but had it clasped between his thumb at the rim and his little finger at the bottom. The old man caught Gil's glance and raised his mug in the air as if he were making a toast.

"Lost all three fingers in a sawmill accident when I was twenty-three. But I've learned I don't need them. Just like Major Powell didn't need his arm to brave the Colorado."

Ten minutes later they were in their red Ford pick-up, washed and vacuumed for the trip, stocked with a two-week supply of food and toilet paper, a pop-up camper in tow.

Gil waved as the truck rolled down the driveway, his eyes on Mr. Pajack's pinky wrapped around the steering wheel. He fully expected not to see them again until the end of August, and he was thoroughly confused when he woke up one morning toward the end of June and saw the pop-up camper sitting in the backyard. At first he thought Jane had miscommunicated with the old couple and they were only planning to be away for a month. His immediate impulse was to withdraw and go home, but Jane put her foot down, claiming that he was doing so well, they couldn't leave yet.

Now, however, in the second week of July, his wife was beginning to unravel. She stood looking out the kitchen window whispering, "This is terrible. This is completely terrible."

"Try to pretend they're not there," Gil said.

"I can't even see the mountains anymore. My eyes can't get past *them*."

"It *is* their backyard. I don't see how we can tell them to leave."

"We gave them three thousand dollars, that's how."

"Technically, that's for the use of the house. I don't know if we legally can lay claim to the backyard."

"We have to do something. We have to."

Gil patted his face with water from the kitchen sink and dried it with the dishtowel. This was all becoming too complicated for him. And Jane was right. He had been doing well. He had been remembering things that he had to remember. He remembered being on the train, just sitting on the train next to a man wearing a brown uniform with a row of pens packed tightly into the chest pocket of his jacket. He remembered squinting for the first few minutes of the ride as the light cut in and out of the car, but then the sun went behind the clouds and his eyes relaxed. He flipped over the newspaper and read that Chile had been stepping up its copper mining and economists feared an inevitable glut of minerals on the world market. Then there was a gap, and then he stopped going to work, but he couldn't remember why.

Gil stepped out onto the porch, the screen door whacking behind him. The sound of it jolted Mr. Pajack, who had been dozing in his lawn chair. He looked up at Gil, then propped his elbow up again and buried his face in his hand. Unlike Jane, Gil was still able to see beyond the Pajacks' camper to the vacant horse farm on the edge of their property. Before the pop-up camper returned, he had fallen into the habit of walking around the empty corrals. Sometimes there would be a light breeze in the evening, and he'd kick the dust up and hold his breath as it floated all around him. He'd climb up to the loft in one of the old, abandoned barns and the dust still would be hovering in the air above the corrals. He'd look out toward the Pajacks' house and imagine there were horses below him, kicking up the dust as they trotted around in circles. He'd sit there until after dark and try to remember the man in the brown uniform on the train. He felt the need to know who he was and he found himself creating a life for him. He began to see him with the horses, dragging his work boots through the dust, feeding them hay or carrots. On some days he'd bring out a saddle or two. Other times he'd just stand there in the middle of the corral with a Morgan or an Arabian, brushing its coat, looking up at Gil in the barn.

He felt confident that one day the man would say something and he would find out who he was, but now, since the Pajacks had camped in the backyard, he'd only gone down to the corrals once. They had constructed a portable commode upon their return, and the one time Gil had walked through the yard on the way to the horse farm he caught Mrs. Pajack squatting behind the pop-up camper. She smiled uneasily at him, the brown paisley dress pulled up to her chest, and he looked away as quickly as he could.

He hadn't walked through the backyard again, and his desire to go back to the horse corrals and see what he would remember made him consider speaking to the Pajacks. He paced back and forth across the porch, the floorboards squeaking with each step, Jane still mumbling to herself in the kitchen, "This is terrible. This is completely terrible."

Mr. Pajack opened one eye, looking up at the house for a second before nodding off again, and Gil leapt down the stairs and stood in front of him. The old man's left thumb and pinky were clasped around the lawn chair's metal armrest and Gil found himself staring at the gap where the fingers used to be.

"Mr. Pajack," he said, speaking to the three small nubs on his hand.

Pajack shifted in his chair, but did not open his eyes. Gil did not repeat himself. He shoved his hands in the pockets of his shorts and looked around the campsite hoping Mrs. Pajack would appear somewhere, but he hadn't seen her all day.

Pajack grunted, one eye half-open. "Mr. Salima. What is it?"

"I think we should have a dialogue about our situation. My wife and I have grown beyond uncomfortable."

"What situation is that, Mr. Salima?"

Gil took a deep breath and looked back at the house. He was losing his nerve and he hoped Jane might at least come out onto the porch for moral support, but she wasn't even in the kitchen window anymore.

"Sit down," Mr. Pajack said, nodding to the chair beside him. "Go 'head. Have a seat."

Gil hesitated, then sat down. Mrs. Pajack's lawn chair wobbled from side to side, and Gil felt as if he were trespassing on intimate property. If she found out, it might be as much of a violation as seeing her go to the bathroom. A couple of the weaved strips were broken, and as he sank into the seat he propped himself up on the armrests, afraid he'd fall straight through to the ground if he let all his weight come to bear on the chair.

Pajack's feet were buried in the lawn, which hadn't been mowed since they'd returned. He pulled out long blades of grass, then spread his toes apart and shook his leg until the grass fell from his foot. He looked up at the sky and rolled his head from side to side, his neck popping as he did so.

Finally, he stretched his arms into the air and yawned, "What's the problem?"

"Jane and I are very uncomfortable with this situation as it's developed."

"I know. There's no reason we shouldn't be speaking to each other. And as far as I'm concerned, Gil, that's all water under the bridge. I picked up some corn on the cob and some blood sausage this morning and you and your wife are more than welcome to join me and mine for dinner."

"That's very hospitable of you. But this is not how we had planned to spend our summer."

"Us either. Thought I'd be in Vegas right now, swimming in my brother-in-law's pool and playing blackjack. How was I to know he'd been gambling away his life's savings?"

"I sympathize with you, but we have a business deal. We've paid you up front. You're neglecting to fulfill your end of the agreement."

"We've rented you our house, not our yard, Mr. Salima. You have nothin' to do with the yard. I've even had the boy down the street mowin' it so you wouldn't have to think about it."

Immobile in the sagging lawn chair, his hands clasped around its pitted metal, Gil found himself being overcome by a numbing paralysis. It was the same sensation he'd felt on the commuter rail. He remembered now that on the train he could feel his legs, but he could not move them. A stream of warmth had run over them, and then he became so cold he was shivering. But still, he could not stand up. All he could do was look out the window at a pile of old tires and rusted automobile parts along the side of the track. He felt guilty for being unable to move. And he wanted to be outside there, behind the power lines and the telephone poles. Inside his head, it was as if someone else were speaking to him, saying, *You need to get out of here, Gilbert. You need to get out.*

He hadn't remembered those thoughts before, and there on the Pajacks' lawn he repeated them out loud, "You need to get out. You need to get out."

"Huh? I ain't goin' anywhere, my friend," Pajack said. "I ain't leavin' this yard. I ain't leavin' this damn chair."

He raised his closed fist in the air and held it out in front of Gil's face. "Now, right now, I'd only have one finger stickin' up if I had said finger. And you know what finger that would be, don't you, Mr. Salima?"

Gil said nothing. He was just happy to have turned his head and faced Pajack. Any kind of movement was progress, and he was sure that anytime now he would be able to pull himself up and go back into the house.

Irene Pajack was not the type of woman to spend the summer in a pop-camper on I-80. Raised in Massachusetts, she had flown to Georgia to visit her son, to Nevada to visit her brother, and to Florida to vacation. But she had never driven farther than Maine, and she wouldn't have made those trips if her father hadn't forced her. At least once every summer during her teens, she sat in the back seat of the family Chevrolet, riddled with nausea and heaving into a bucket, her father looking in the rearview mirror, saying "Make sure it all goes in the pail! This is a new car."

Over the years, she'd built up her stamina. She was able to take leisurely drives with Merrill along the Mohawk trail and enjoy the leaves changing colors in fall. She'd even rode three hours to a lake in New York

State that Merrill had wanted to visit. But the idea of driving cross-country was one she never wanted to consider. Ever since her brother had moved to Las Vegas, Merrill had coaxed her with the notion that it would be like another honeymoon. She had managed to avoid the issue, but when he came home one day with the camper in tow, she knew her years of resistance were about to end.

So, during the first week of June, with great reservation, she climbed into the cab of the pick-up, blessed herself, and said to Merrill, "Pappa, don't stop until we get to Nevada." But they'd turned back in Wyoming, after ten days on the road. Eight days later, they were back in Amherst, their three-month trip shortened to less than three weeks. She was saddened because Merrill was so disappointed, but she couldn't hide the fact that she was relieved to be home. All the way from Illinois, she had been daydreaming about stretching out on the king-size bed she and Merrill had gotten a year ago. It was so big, they had to move their bureaus to another room so it could fit in the bedroom. If she and Merrill each were lying on one side of the bed they would have to reach as far as they could to touch each other, and even then only their fingertips touched.

Irene didn't remember the Salimases until she saw their car parked in the driveway at three o'clock in the morning. When Merrill pulled up to the house, the first thing she thought of was the young couple making love on her bed, and the image she had was of Jane Salimas on top.

"Merrill, my God, the Salimases are here," she whispered to her husband. "What are we going to do?"

Merrill stopped the truck at the front curb and sat quietly for a second. Then he put the truck in gear again and pulled into the driveway. He was heading straight for the Salimases' Volvo, but swerved around it and rolled the truck out into the backyard.

"Merrill, the lawn!" Irene said, but she could see that he was determined. He jammed the pick-up in park, got out to detach the camper, then pulled the truck forward and cut the engine. Irene followed him as he climbed into the camper, and, without a word, pushed out the flaps and went to sleep. But she sat up for a long time, looking out the screened window at the house, silent and dark, two strangers living in it.

For days she tried to pretend she was comfortable out in the trailer, but she couldn't stand the thought of spending the rest of the summer in the backyard while someone else stayed in her house. Often, she sat in her lawn chair watching the house to see if she could track the Salimases' movement.

Gil Salimas was much less visible than his wife. He seemed to spend much of his time upstairs in one of the spare bedrooms. Irene didn't know what he did up there, but she watched him screw the blinds closed every afternoon and then open them again at around five o'clock. And, of course, the two of them slept in the master bedroom, the curtains always drawn across the windows.

The Salimases could be seen most in the kitchen, where Irene had a clear view of their heads as they walked by the window above the sink. In the afternoon, when Jane Salimas prepared lunch, she stood right there in the window, and Irene listened to the water run and the sound of vegetables being peeled. The idea of someone else using the cutting board her father had made or the teapot her grandmother had bequeathed to her irked Irene more than she ever expected it would. "Make yourselves at home," she'd told them before she and Merrill had left. But she never imagined what it would be like to listen to a strange woman handle her pots and pans.

The worst of it was when Jane Salimas came out onto the porch. For some unexplainable reason, they had brought the recycling bin outside and put it near the steps. They also had moved the wicker chairs from one side of the porch to the other and made no attempt to put them back after the Pajacks returned home. Every so often, Jane Salimas would come out, throw a bottle into the bin, then sit down on one of the chairs for a few minutes, as if she were asserting her authority over a domain that was not her own. Irene would stare at her and say to herself over and over again, "Leave my house. Leave my house."

She bored quickly of Merrill's routine of hibachi dinners and cards at the picnic table every night. She began to take walks after dark, to stretch her legs and enjoy the cool night air. When she got close enough to the house, she could see what the Salimases were doing if they were downstairs. In the beginning, she would just pass by the living room window and glance out of the corner of her eye. But after a while she became challenged by the idea of slowing down and eventually stopping in front of a window, without being caught.

She would circle the house several times in an evening, and once she swore Gil Salimas stared right at her, but they never made an effort to close the curtains so Irene figured she was safe. She liked to pretend she had the house under siege, as if she were waiting outside the gates of Troy. No one got in or out, and it would only be a matter of time before she found a way to vanquish her foe.

Merrill Pajack had had his doubts about Gil Salimas.
"There's something weird with that guy," he had said to his wife as

they pulled away from the house during the first week of June. "There's something wrong with him, Irene. I just don't know what it is."

But he was content to have pocketed $3,000, which would put them well on their way to financing a trip cross-country in a pop-up camper. His brother, Angus, had told him he could get more than a $1,000 a month for such a house in Amherst. But, Merrill was confident that, whatever Gil Salimas' condition was, the couple he'd just rented to would be a lot less likely to throw parties or invite other people into his home.

"You locked up the good silverware, right?" he said to his wife somewhere on I-90 in upstate New York.

"And the china, too," she said.

By the time they were in Ohio, Merrill no longer thought of the Salimases back in Amherst. He was focused on the trip at hand and getting to Wyoming as soon as possible. He had wanted to drive twelve hours a day, but grudgingly slowed their pace after Irene began vomiting in a paper bag as they sped through Cleveland.

He had sympathy for his wife, but wanted to get to Green River and spend some time there before they began the journey to Irene's brother's place in Nevada. For years, he had envisioned this trip with its stop to salute John Wesley Powell. He'd read all the books he could find about the expedition the one-armed Major led down the Green and Colorado Rivers. All the hardships he and his men suffered were well documented in Merrill's mind. Their wooden boats were smashed and had to be rebuilt. Several times they nearly drowned. They almost starved, too, once becoming severely ill after eating rancid bacon. In fear of the unknown that lay ahead in the Grand Canyon, two of the crew abandoned the others, only to be killed by Indians as they tried to save themselves. Through it all, though, Major Powell, undaunted by his handicap, held the rest of the expedition together and led them to safety.

Merrill was on his own expedition now, and, through the long hours on I-80, he imagined what kind of monument had been erected in Major Powell's honor where his journey had begun in the town of Green River, Wyoming. He imagined a life-size bronze statue of the Major holding his hat in one hand, his other arm conspicuously missing. He imagined a crowd of people gathered around the monument, standing quietly, a woman or two placing flowers at the Major's feet. He imagined there'd be a big museum with replicas of the small boats that were used for the expedition and pieces of the original oars that had been broken into pieces. There would be a souvenir shop where he could buy Irene a key chain to remember the trip. There would be a hot dog stand, and they would sit there eating hot dogs, looking down the Green River, imagining what it looked like when it merged into the Colorado.

He had expected to see big signs pointing the way to the Powell monument when they pulled off the highway in Wyoming, but none were to be found. Merrill stopped at an old gas station and had to ask for directions three times before the attendant figured out what he was talking about.

Irene said they should go to the campground to rest and shower before visiting the monument. She said the cab of the truck stunk like the time Merrill broke his leg and hadn't showered or left the bedroom for two weeks. But Merrill wouldn't hear of it. He was determined to see the Powell Memorial while the sun was still high in the sky.

"Besides," he told her, "the Major didn't shower on his expedition."

"The Major was not a fool," she said. "He jumped in the river when his first mate complained of B.O."

Merrill ignored her, and, following the gas station attendant's instructions, he found his way down to an old cobblestone bridge where he stopped the truck to take a picture of a wooden sign that had etched into it: JOHN WESLEY POWELL EXPEDITION ISLAND.

"This is it, Irene," he said. "This is it."

He could not suppress the smile on his face. This moment gave him a sense of purpose quite unlike anything he had ever experienced before.

"We have arrived," he said, stepping on the gas pedal.

Irene's head knocked against the back window as the truck rambled over the short bridge, crossing a small inlet of murky water. Merrill pulled into one of ten empty parking spaces. He hadn't seen another car since they left the main road by the gas station.

He hopped out of the truck and surveyed the little island. It was about two hundred yards long, lined with trees and tall grasses along the riverbank that blocked his view of the water. A solitary picnic table with a cracked bench sat in a clearing, the sun shining brightly on it, dandelions and other weeds sprung up all around it.

He walked across the parking lot to a padlocked little shack that had a sign on the door identifying it as the John Wesley Powell Expedition museum, open Mondays from noon to five, July through August. He pushed at the door and it gave a little, but the padlock only allowed for an inch or so of movement. He put his eye to the crack and strained to see whatever there was to see, but the room was too dark. He kicked the door and looked for a way in through a window, but they were boarded shut.

The museum wasn't important, he decided, as long as he could see the spot where John Wesley Powell had launched his expedition. He followed a gravel path through the trees to the river, where he assumed the replica of the Major would have been built. But when he reached the clearing all he found was another wooden plaque atop a thin pole. It said, "Here began the Powell Expedition down the Green and Colorado Rivers, 1869." Scattered at the foot of the plaque were cigarette butts, broken Budweiser bottles, and a small pile of chicken bones, completely cleaned of the skin and meat, flies buzzing around them. A breeze picked up ashes from a recent campfire and blew them onto the river's smooth current, where they floated downstream until Merrill could not see them anymore.

He bent down and ran his hands through the water, feeling how cold it was. He patted his face and wiped the sweat from his forehead. Then he sat back against a tree trunk and watched the river pass him by. Only then did he realize the Green River was a dusty, gray color. He closed his eyes and tried to make an imprint of this scene on his mind. He wanted to be able to remember it, along with the sense of failure that it seemed to give him. The river rolled by him with hardly a sound. He crossed his arms over his knees and smelled something terrible, but he wasn't sure if it was the mud by the water or his own body odor.

When he got back to the truck, Irene was sleeping, laid out across the seat, her head by the steering wheel. He woke her and told her he'd just as soon skip Las Vegas and go home now. She protested, saying that they had gone this far and she didn't care if she threw up every hour on the hour, she was going to make it to Las Vegas. But she stopped arguing when they called her brother and he said the bank was repossessing his house and he couldn't guarantee they'd have a place to stay if they came.

In the morning, they were back on I-80, heading east.

A heat wave rolled in around the tenth of July, and while the high temperatures made the Pajacks restless, the Salimases became lethargic. They spent most of their time downstairs where ceiling fans in the kitchen and dining room circulated the air better than the smaller fans upstairs. Gil Salimas had even taken to sleeping on the couch in the living room, which Jane considered a step backwards in the normalization of their relationship.

They hadn't made love since March, and whenever she touched him he still gave her that look of bewilderment, as if he didn't know her. He didn't resist or pull away, but she couldn't help but feel like a stranger, and her efforts at affection had dwindled to a minimum.

A month after Gil began seeing a shrink, she started seeing him, too, in separate sessions. He had told her to be patient in the beginning.

There was no need to rock the boat. Her husband was recovering nicely. But, later, the shrink had changed his tune, telling her that some assertiveness on her part might help the situation, as long as she wasn't overly aggressive if Gil was resistant.

She lay on the king-size bed, thinking of this. It was too early and too hot to sleep, but she'd gone upstairs after Gil had shut the lights off and sprawled out on the couch. She got up and paced back and forth in the bedroom, then went into the studio room.

There were three bedrooms upstairs. One they shared, and usually slept in. The second room was Gil's, where, at least once a day, he listened to the self-esteem tapes his mother had given to him, repeating over and over again: "I like myself unconditionally. I like myself unconditionally." And the third room Jane had converted into a studio for her art work.

She never thought of herself as much of an artist, but she'd come to Amherst with the idea of returning to her painting just for relaxation. The day after they arrived, she'd even bought two easels and a few canvases at a store in town. Gil had gone with her and loaded the easels into the back of the Volvo. Then he'd carried them into the house, knocking them against the banister as he went upstairs. "Careful!" she'd said. "Nothing in this house can easily be replaced."

He'd set them down in the bedroom where the Pajacks kept most of their clothes, one easel in front of each bureau. Jane kept them where he left them, mounted two canvases, and began working on two paintings at a time. The first one was a panoramic attempt of the horse corrals with the Berkshires in the background. The second was a close-up of the horse corrals. But after the Pajacks returned, when she could no longer look out the window, she put aside one of the original projects and began work on a painting of two old people playing cards at a picnic table, a clothesline and a pop-up camper in the background. The picture was not flattering. Jane distorted the body parts of the old people, giving them heads and feet that were disproportionately large. The man wore no shirt and had patches of gray hair on his shoulder and forearm. The woman had a cigar hanging from her mouth, wisps of smoke the same color as her hair rising above her head.

Jane had named the painting *The Pajacks Play Pinochle*, and Gil had chuckled when she told him, but she knew he'd squirmed privately, afraid the Pajacks would see it when the Salimases finally moved out. But now, as Jane looked at it, it struck her as more funny than vicious. Everyone is potential material for the amateur artist, she thought to herself. The Pajacks were no exception.

She considered doing some more work on one of the paintings, but another idea entered her head. An antique mirror sat in one corner of the room, supported by a mahogany stand. The mirror was tilted upward so that she could only see the top half of her body, but she noticed her face was flushed from the heat. She liked the way it looked. She regularly complained about the pale features she'd inherited from her parents, but out here in Amherst her skin seemed to have darkened, even if only temporarily. She adjusted the mirror so that she could see her whole body. Then she tied her T-shirt in a knot above her navel and ran her fingers through her hair. She brought no lingerie with her to Massachusetts, but decided it wouldn't make any difference.

Despite the Pajacks, Gil Salimas still found he was making progress in Amherst. He had been sitting up, watching a public television documentary about trains with no adverse reactions, when his wife came downstairs and climbed on top of him. She was on her knees, her chest pressed against his face and her fingers massaging his head.

"I feel like you've been gone for so long," she said.

"Me too," he said, the words muffled under her weight. For the first time in months he wrapped his arms around her and held her.

The narrator of the train documentary was saying, "After falling into less and less use during the golden age of the automobile, trains are now making a comeback. High-speed rail and commuter rail are now seen as essential in the fight against air pollution and automobile traffic."

Gil had thought about that on the train while sitting next to the man with the pens packed into his jacket pocket. He and Jane had often talked about moving, and he hoped they could find a place close to a station so he could take the rail into the city. He liked the idea of Jane picking him up every day and imagined the anticipation he would have looking for the Volvo after work. He wondered if the man next to him was picked up every day by his own wife. He imagined the man saying good-bye to his wife in the morning as she tucked the pens in his pocket in an arrangement that suited her. And, as Gil thought of this, he glanced at the pens and noticed that one of them had leaked. A dark spot had soaked the man's jacket just underneath the pocket.

He was glad to remember this detail and he kissed his wife's breasts. As he did this, she let out a piercing scream and stood straight up on the couch, stepping on his legs. She reached out and slammed the window shut, which dulled the sound of another woman's scream on the outside. Gil turned around just in time to see Mrs. Pajack's white face, eyes wide, mouth open, before she fell off the metal bucket she stood on and rolled through the azaleas on her way to the backyard.

After the Peeping Tom incident, as Jane called it, the Pajacks had moved their lawn chairs to the other side of the pop-up camper where the Salimases couldn't see them, and Gil hadn't heard a sound out of them in three days. He thought perhaps the worst was over and he decided to try to get used to this arrangement for the rest of the summer. By August, he thought, he might even venture down to the horse corrals again.

Jane, on the other hand, had been acting as if she were preparing for an assault on the house. She had gone to the Stop & Shop twice in two days and bought enough groceries to last a month. She hadn't even asked Gil for help carrying the bags in, and instead of bringing them through the front door, which was closer to the car, she brought them around the back so the Pajacks could see that not only did she have no intention of leaving, but she was fortifying her position.

"Now there's nothing they can do to oust us from this house," she said, shoving salmon steaks, frozen waffles, and a five-pound package of lean ground beef into the freezer. Gil wasn't sure if she was talking to him or herself. "I'm gonna sleep in that old lady's bed until it's time to pack the car up and go," she said. "I'm gonna lie naked in it until noon on August thirty-first."

For his part, Gil would have been willing to try to smooth things over with the Pajacks one last time, but Jane wouldn't hear of it. Any benevolent gesture, she said, would be a sign of weakness in the eyes of the enemy. She could not support weakness. She continued to slam foodstuffs around in the kitchen while intermittently checking to see if the Pajacks were paying any attention out in the backyard.

Gil quietly wandered upstairs to his den. He shut the blinds and lay down on the twin bed. Then he placed the headphones from his portable cassette player over his ears and pressed the play button. His mother had given him several sets of "relaxation tapes," and Gil was to listen to one every day, meditating on the words or the sounds. Each tape varied in its content. Sometimes they were quiet, peaceful sounds, with labels like "The Pacific Ocean off the Coast of Kauai," or "Bird Sounds Along the Purus River in the Brazilian Rainforest." Sometimes they were soothing voices, telling stories, or creating vivid images that Gil's mind was supposed to latch onto, images that would take him away from the present moment to another time and place. Sometimes the tapes even encouraged him to pretend he was another person for an hour or so. These personality cassettes all began the same way. Gil's favorite was the Walt Whitman tape, which said *I am Walt Whitman, bard of America. I celebrate myself, and sing myself.* At different times throughout the summer he had been Thomas Jefferson, Albert Einstein, and Queen Elizabeth I.

The tape he listened to now was entitled "The Well of the Soul," and the voice was of a man who spoke softly, but confidently, like Gil's sixth grade teacher. *You are in a well. A deep well, but you can see the blue sky above you, and you know you can be lifted out at any time. You want to be there. You like the sound of water dripping peacefully from above.*

The man's voice was interrupted by what sounded like a leaky shower head.

Dark, gray rock surrounds you, rising all the way up the cylindrical well to the sky. You are sitting in water that rises up to your chest, but it is warm water, and it is soothing, relaxing every muscle in your body until you feel light and free. You close your eyes and imagine that you are Mozart composing your own music in this den of tranquility.

The dripping sounds in the background gave way to a selection of classical music, and the voice disappeared. Gil no longer heard Jane clanking around in the kitchen, but after a few minutes she was shouting to him from the base of the stairs.

"I'm going out for one last canvas," she said. "Make sure you keep the doors locked."

Keep the doors locked? Gil thought to himself. What are they going to do, break into their own house? They have keys for goodness sake.

He turned the volume up on the tape player so that he couldn't hear anything else. The voice came on and off randomly, speaking over the music. *There is no one in your well but you. You have complete control in your well. There is nothing to thwart you. There is nothing to disturb your tranquility.*

By the time he flipped the tape over, his thoughts had wandered to the train. It seemed that every time he shut his eyes now he saw out the train window. Telephone lines stretched along the tracks, carried by poles that were tilted toward the ground in one direction or another. Row houses stood less than fifty yards away, made from red brick that had turned moldy green all the way up to the second floor. Their rusty fire escapes seemed to rattle and shake as the train rumbled by. Then the train stopped before it reached the next station.

The man with the pens, sitting to the left of Gil, seemed to be looking outside the train, too. His head was resting against the window and Gil noticed that the spot on his jacket had grown larger.

When you leave the well, you will feel refreshed and your soul will feel redeemed, the voice on the tape was saying. *You will feel healed and you will be stronger, able to take on any challenges that lie before you.*

The Mozart music became loud again, closing Gil off to everything beyond the headphones. He didn't even hear the clap of Mrs. Pajack's heavy footsteps as she rushed up the stairs. He didn't hear a thing until she slammed the easels down to the hardwood floor in the other room, and even then he thought what he heard was gunfire. He didn't even know someone else was upstairs until she stood in front of him, trying to tear apart one of Jane's paintings with her bare hands.

Merrill Pajack did not catch up to his wife until she stood above Gil Salimas, cowering in a fetal position on the floor, personal headphones dangling from his hand.

Merrill dove for Irene just as she ran underneath the clothesline in the backyard, but all he did was trip her up a bit. Before he got to his feet again she was already in the house screaming wildly, "I want her out! Get her out of my house!"

She had stopped in the kitchen, pulled Jane Salimas' five pounds of ground beef from the freezer and slammed it to the floor. Then she ran through the dining and living rooms, knocking over chairs and whatever possessions of the Salimases she found. When Merrill stepped into the house, she heaved a set of keys at him and they went right out the door, sliding across the porch to the overgrown lawn.

"Irene! Just stop before you go any further," he said.

She stood there for a moment, panting, her fists clenched. Then she shouted "I want her out of my house!" again and bolted up the stairs.

When Merrill reached the back bedroom and saw Gil Salimas on the floor, he thought for sure that his wife had killed him. But then he heard Gil mumbling to himself and he was relieved that the man was conscious. Irene had quieted down now except for the wheezing that rose and fell in sync with her chest. She hovered above Gil with a frightened look on her face—the same kind of pasty look she had while vomiting her way through Ohio.

Merrill got down on one knee and leaned in close to Gil. "Mr. Salima?" he said.

"Oh, God, it's blood," Gil was mumbling. He said something else, but Merrill couldn't make out what it was, then he repeated, "It's blood. It's blood."

"Where?" Merrill had taken the headphones from his hand and was trying to roll him over to see if there was blood underneath him. "Where? I don't see any?"

"Check the back of his head," Irene said.

Merrill reached around and touched Gil's hair, but there was nothing. "I don't see anything," he said, looking at his wife.

Gil Salimas grabbed his hand with the missing fingers and squeezed it tightly. "I think he's been shot," he said. He was trying to get back into his well, but he kept imagining the sound of gunshots and he couldn't hear the dripping water anymore. The man with the pens was slumped beside him. He wanted to touch him, to see if he was alive, but he sat there frozen, watching people run past him, exiting the train as quickly as possible.

"What's he talking about?" Irene said.

"I can't get back in my well," Gil said, staring up at Merrill.

"I don't know," Merrill said to his wife. "What did you do to him?"

"Nothing! Nothing. He fell on the floor as soon as I walked in."

"I think he's dead. He's dead!" Gil was saying.

Merrill looked at Irene and noticed her lip was quivering like it did every time just before she asked him to pull over on the side of the road.

"Go to the bathroom!" he said to her, and she ran out of the room, holding her hand over her mouth.

"I am John Wesley Powell, conqueror of the great Colorado," Gil was saying, as if the Major had been one of the characters on his relaxation tapes. "I beat that river with only one arm."

Merrill looked at Gil as if he had committed blasphemy. "I think he's on drugs," he shouted to Irene, who had no response. "He was a good man, Mr. Salima. He got farther than you or I ever will."

For a minute there was silence in the room, except for the sound of Irene retching in the bathroom. Gil tried to get a better grip on Merrill's hand by wrapping his fingers around his thumb. He pulled on the thumb and brought himself up into a sitting position. The two men were face to face, close enough so that Merrill could feel Gil's breath on his cheek, and an uneasy feeling came over Merrill. It was the same thing he felt while sitting there on Expedition Island: his search for one redeeming moment still eluded him.

"I need to get out of here," Gil whispered. "Take me out of here."

Irene lifted her head from the toilet bowl just in time to see Merrill walk by carrying Gil Salimas in his arms. She had no idea her husband was strong enough to do such a thing, and she feared she'd hear a crash and the two of them would go tumbling down the stairs. But Merrill's footsteps remained steady until she heard him kick the screen door open and go outside.

She flushed the toilet, but stayed there on the bathroom floor, leaning against the vanity for a long while. Jane Salimas' cosmetics were neatly piled on top of the toilet tank in a small wicker basket. The arrangement looked like a bouquet of flowers, with colorful bottles interspersed between cucumber green ones. At the top of the pile, she noticed a little pink bottle of moisturizing cream with fancy black letters written across it, spelling out words she never could pronounce correctly: *Yves Saint Laurent*. Once, when she still worked in the chancellor's office at the state university, she had been given the same bottle for Christmas by her boss. She had loved how smooth it made her skin feel, but later, when she went to buy more, she was appalled to find the little bottle was so expensive. She was determined not to buy it until her skin became very old and very scaly and she really needed it. Secretly, though, she hoped Merrill would get it for her someday.

For a second she wondered what Merrill was doing with Gil Salimas out in the backyard, but then she grabbed the bottle and pumped it several times into her hand. She spread the pale lotion all over her neck and face. There was too much of it and her skin couldn't absorb it, so she wiped the excess on her arms, and then her chest, pushing her fingers inside her bra.

She felt like an intruder in her own house and began to feel giddy with the anticipation of being caught using another woman's lotion. Then, when she turned to leave, Jane Salimas stood there in the doorway, the five-pound package of ground beef in her hands.

"Where's my husband?" she said.

"Outside," Irene said, her voice quiet, "with Merrill." She looked down at the *Yves Saint Laurent* she'd left on the sink, out of its place.

Jane stepped toward Mrs. Pajack. Irene backed up against the wall. The meat was dripping. Red dots lined the bathroom floor, and Jane put the package down on the toilet seat so it would drip into the bowl. The two women stood in silence for a moment, then Jane raised the blinds and looked out the window for the first time since June.

Dusk was setting in, and from the bathroom the Berkshires looked like dark shadows in the distance. Jane listened for them, her face pressed up against the sagging window screen, but all she heard was the slow drip of the juice from the meat falling into the toilet water. Her thoughts were clear, clearer than they had been in a long time. And she thought she should say something profound to Mrs. Pajack, something that would sum up the experience of this summer in Amherst, something that the woman would remember for years to come.

But all that came out of her mouth was: "It's not *Yves Saint Laurent*. I just saved the bottle and refilled it with Vaseline Intensive Care."

Irene looked at her, trying to memorize how Jane pronounced *Yves Saint Laurent* so she could ask for it by name. She was sixty-four, and there was no point in waiting any longer.

Down below, the pick-up truck was moving slowly across the yard, Merrill at the wheel, Gil sitting in a lawn chair atop the flatbed, facing back toward the house. The two women watched as the truck glided down to the corrals, Gil's head bouncing about over the bumps. Without saying anything, Jane and Irene seemed to share the same fear—that the lawn chair would collapse and Gil would roll off the flatbed and be knocked unconscious before Merrill even knew what happened. But the chair stayed upright, and the truck entered the corrals, hugging the edge of the fence and circling around and around until thick clouds of dust rose up over the barn.

The dust still had not settled by the time the women made their way down to the center of the corral where the truck had parked. Merrill was standing, leaning against one of the wheel wells, facing Gil, who still sat in the lawn chair atop the pick-up.

"Appaloosas, Morgans, a few Arabians," Merrill was saying. "They must have had thirty-five horses here at one point."

"Did you ride?" Gil said.

"No," Merrill chuckled. "I just sat up on the porch and watched 'em trot around."

Gil was looking across the corral. He saw nothing but empty dust hovering above the ground. He kept his mouth closed, trying not to inhale it, but the air had turned crisp and soon he was taking deep breaths. And the more he took in the cool air, the more confident he became. He knew it would only take another ten or fifteen minutes—maybe twenty—and then he would be able to stand up.

Plateau

You've been traveling on a bus with thirty-five fifteen-year-olds for over a month now, sampling cities and national parks of the American West. You pull into a campground somewhere near the Grand Canyon, though you can only take the bus driver's word that the Canyon is nearby because you've never been to Arizona and you didn't actually see the Canyon during the drive in.

The tents are up quickly, and you feel satisfied because these kids have never put up tents before (except for the ones they may have made by draping blankets over La-Z-Boy chairs in their parents' living rooms in New Jersey) and they finally seem to be getting the hang of it. But soon, in the great tradition of the MTV age, they are off to the IMAX theater to watch a film *about* the Grand Canyon. It is the evening of the only night you will spend here, and the only time they actually will have along the Canyon Rim is between sunrise and nine o'clock the next morning (when they'll be walking zombies at best, if they don't decide to sleep in altogether), then they're off to Utah. So, essentially, they have traveled across the desert to see a movie.

You, on the other hand, have volunteered for grocery duty, because, unless you're fortunate enough to be driving the Ryder truck loaded with all the camping equipment, grocery duty is the only opportunity you have to be alone on any given day. And you like the kids well enough, but you're the type that needs solitude. You long for grocery duty, you bribe the other counselors so you can do the shopping. So, as soon as the kids are whisked away on the bus, off to the theater, you're off to the market.

Of course, you find it terribly odd that there's a supermarket right here at the Grand Canyon.

You're conservative, gathering food that you're confident fifteen-year-olds will eat: hot dogs, Cinnamon Toast Crunch, watermelon, enough ingredients for lasagna because the cook's decided to get creative on the open range during the last weeks of the trip. And while you're looking for tomato sauce and ground beef, it occurs to you that this whole Grand Canyon thing could be a myth. It might not exist. It's a tourist trap, that once initiated into, you're sworn to promote despite its non-existence. You've already heard several foreign languages being spoken. You're not sure what they are, but you guess German, Italian, French, maybe. People have come from all over the world, seduced by this myth. But the Grand Canyon really is just a grocery store hidden in a forest of ponderosa pines, in the American Southwest, in the middle of nowhere.

You finish shopping more quickly than you expected you would, pleased with yourself because even you are getting the hang of this. The kids can set up tents and you could plan meals for forty people if you had to. Back at camp, you tuck all the food away, still fearful of the raccoons that everyone back in New Jersey warned would devour anything left unprotected, even though the only animal you've seen up-close on this trip has been a cow that stood staring at you somewhere off the road in Iowa when you stopped to use the bathroom.

Dusk is approaching. The kids are still not due back for a while. You are free. This is the only moment you've had to do nothing but be alone with yourself since one of the teenagers became ill in San Francisco and you volunteered to stay in the hotel room adjoining his all day, whispering to him through the door every hour, "Heath? Heath, are you okay? Do you still feel sick?"

The Grand Canyon has never captured your imagination that much. You've read books. You've seen photographs, you suppose. You even took a geology course in college where the professor spent two weeks talking about why "the great Chasm of the Colorado is the most significant geological location on Earth." You listened to most of his lectures. But the Canyon's been relegated to the status of cliché for you. The Tetons were your thing, you thought. You'd never heard of them. You snapped forty-two pictures of those iron, July-snowcapped mountains from a moving bus. The Canyon might be one of the bigger holes in the Earth, but it couldn't compare to the Tetons. Nonetheless, you've traveled across a scorched desert, and there really is no question about what you should do while you're here. You have to see this supposedly grand attraction and judge for yourself. At the very least you'll find out if there's really more to it than the grocery store.

You start out in a slow jog because darkness is coming and you're still not sure which way the Canyon is. You go along on one trail for a while, passing through pine after pine after pine. It's unpleasant for you because you've always equated the smell of pine needles with the first time you ever got drunk, siphoning a cheap bottle of gin stashed underneath the kitchen sink at your parents' house. The smell of the gin. The smell of the vomit. Then quietly trying to wash your sheets at four in the morning, praying you won't wake up your parents. There was nothing redeeming about the experience, aside from the fact that you've never touched gin since. But the pines bring it all back to you, and for the first time since you've been out West, you think you might miss home. How stupid, you think, though. You've been traveling through some of the most incredible landscape in the world. Why should an episode of puking make you homesick? Home is the worn Appalachians. Home is East. You've read that, geologically speaking, the western part of the continent is much younger than the eastern half. In millions of years the Tetons are going to look like the Berkshires. Nice, but not impressive. And you want impressive. When the Tetons become worn-down and eroded, the West will no longer be the West. Better to have the oceans sweep over the continent again than to endure the sheer inevitability of old age, you think. Better to drown than see the Grand Tetons flattened.

You stay on the trail for a ways but you just keep cutting through more and more campsites. You must be going the wrong way. "Hey," you say to a man with no shirt on who's rummaging through the trunk of his car, "which way's the Canyon?"

Even to you, your question sounds ludicrous. The biggest hole in the United States and you can't find it. Some explorer you would be. Right up there with John Wesley Powell, braving the entire Colorado in a wooden boat even after losing an arm in the Civil War. But the guy without the shirt doesn't mock you. "Back that way and left," he says, pointing in the direction from which you just came.

So, you go back that way and left, picking up your pace now because the sun is getting ready to set, and you figure, what the hell, *sunset at the Grand Canyon*. If it's any good you can tell the kids about it. Hell, if it's that good you can bring your own children here. If it's incredible like people say, you can make a yearly thing of it. Canyon trip at the end of June every year. Pack up the kids in the Isuzu Trooper right after school gets out and just drive. If you ever have kids. If you ever get married.

Finally, you spot a building that looks like a ranger station, or at least a public rest room. Next to it is a wooden sign staked into the ground with the words "Canyon Rim" and an arrow pointing straight ahead. You wonder how much farther. If it weren't for that sign you'd still have no idea where to find this big spectacle. You've hiked the Tetons, you've hiked Yosemite, Yellowstone. You thought you were in pretty good shape, but this run to the Canyon, across paved, flat land, is taking the breath out of you. Your chest is tight, heaving. You want to stop, but darkness is on the way, the kids are on the way. You don't have much time; you have to get back. You consider giving up and just returning to your campsite, but you've come this far, and deep down you know you'll be a zombie yourself in the morning. If the Canyon is worth seeing, you've got to see it now.

So you run on, rows of pines standing on each side of you, slapping your feet loudly into the asphalt path that winds around into more trees ahead of you. You see no opening, no clearing. Just forest. You're passing people who are walking in the same direction, cameras slung around their shoulders, lawn chairs in hand, backpacks on their backs. Your feet slap past them. They're carrying jackets, or wearing sweaters. You're sweating. Your eyes burning from perspiration.

And then you hit it. The trees run out and you can see the sky ahead. You run right into a huge expanse of space, and it's the space that stops you, like you've run into a lead wall. And you're thankful for the space for holding you back because you feel lighter than you've ever felt, and you're not close enough to look down yet, but you know if the air didn't stop your momentum you'd fall for nearly two billion years.

You have heard that at least one person per year stands on the Rim of the Grand Canyon, swoons, and tumbles over the edge to their death. You think about sitting down, just to be on the safe side, but your knees don't want to bend and you'd just as well not move at all. You try to keep completely still, but then you can feel it. You don't want to, but you've got no control over it: your face is cracking into a smile. You try to stop and look around you. You don't want anybody to see this. But you can't help it, you're giggling. Giggling at the Grand Canyon.   You try to stop yourself and you mumble something, something that sounds like *gulash*, or *galosh*, you're not sure which, though neither seems appropriate. But just what would be appropriate?

A strong breeze blows against your back, strong enough to push you a step closer to the brink. This is enough to make you sit down now, Indian-style, all your weight on your feet so they won't get the idea to stand up again until you're good and ready. You compose yourself for a minute and then realize you've shut your eyes. This is the greatest scene you could ever see, you think to yourself. This is why God gave you eyes, so one day you could come here and finally "Be still, and know that I am God." You have heard that the Hopis believe there's a spot in the Canyon along the bank of the river where life began, where humans first entered the world. You get the feeling that if only you could open your eyes you could unlock all the mysteries of life that have plagued you, seemingly more than they plague other people. But maybe that's why your eyes are closed. Maybe you're afraid of what you'll find. The answers must be down there somewhere, hidden among those two billion years of exposed Earth history, down through the Permian period, then the Carboniferous, then the Devonian, and then the missing Silurian and Ordovician that followed the Cambrian. Then on down to the oldest of the old, the Precambrian, containing the bottommost layer of rock: the dark Vishnu Schist.

"What is a Vishnu Schist?" you'd asked the geology professor.

"The bottommost layer of rock," he answered. "It may have witnessed the first life."

But that wasn't what you wanted to know. You wanted to know what Vishnu Schist *meant*. Was it somebody's name? Was it a different language? You were willing to bet that *schist* meant *rock*, and you thought you'd heard the word *Vishnu* someplace before, but you couldn't place it. You halfheartedly looked through your geology text for the answer, but all you learned was that the Vishnu Schist was named in 1890 by one C.D. Walcott. And if he was still alive you probably would have tried to contact him in hope he could answer your question. But, since he wasn't, you relegated Vishnu Schist to the status of a derogatory term because you liked the sound of it. You began to use it on your friends whenever they annoyed you. "Don't be such a Vishnu Schist," you'd say. Nobody knew what you meant, not even you.

For years, you never could recall where you'd heard the word Vishnu before Geology 101. But now, standing on the Rim of the Grand Canyon, somehow you remember. Vishnu is a part of the Hindu Trinity. Brahma, Vishnu, and Shiva. Suddenly you feel like a blasphemer. You feel ashamed, and it is the Canyon that has shamed you, with its peaks—Isis, Odin, Osiris, Horus—rising up from the inner gorge.

"Oh, my," you hear a woman say behind you. "Oh, my. My, my, my, my, my."

You open your eyes and look out into the colors of the sky, hovering just above the colors of the rock. You have heard of people who have an unusual disease, the technical term for which you cannot remember, that affects their semicircular canals so that at any given moment they can completely lose their balance and become uncontrollably dizzy. You think that, for people afflicted with that illness, this may be the only place on the planet where they could stand up straight and walk confidently in complete equilibrium. You, on the other hand, are experiencing vertigo.

You shut your eyes again and keep them closed for a long while. You smell the pines, you feel the breeze, you hear people walking by, you can feel their presence, but all that seems so distant now. The Canyon is spread out before you, two hundred miles long, fifteen miles wide, one mile deep, descending through layer upon layer of time. You try to imagine what it looks like, even though it's right there in front of you. Then, when you finally open your eyes again, it's gone. Darkness has enveloped the entire landscape. You know you're on the Rim, a few feet away from oblivion, but you can't imagine it. Somehow, you feel you could step over the edge and just keep on walking across the darkness, across the abyss, across time and space. But you can't imagine what would be there on the other side.

*   *   *

Back at camp, the kids say the movie was good. "It was like we were floating through the Grand Canyon in stereo," they say. "What'd you do while we were gone?" they ask.

"Nothing," you say. "Just got groceries and hung around," you say, wondering if they experienced the Canyon more through a movie than you did on the Rim. Maybe that was the only way to experience it. Pictures and film reduced it to something comprehensible, something that you could actually look at.

"What time does the sun rise?" somebody asks. You're not sure. You're not sure that the sun rises here at the same time as the rest of the Southwest. You're not even sure if the sun rises here. How could it?

"Early," one of the other counselors says. "Early, so don't stay up all night."

These kids staying up all night has not been a problem, you think to yourself. The days have been so long and so tiring, so packed with driving, and sightseeing, and eating, that they are actually glad to lie down on air mattresses and sleep outside. Tonight is no exception. By eleven o'clock the tents are quiet. You're sitting with the other counselors in the back of the Ryder truck—your usual meeting place to gripe about the kids, talk about which ones are homesick, or which ones have gotten and given hickeys right under your noses.

You can't bring yourself to tell the others what you did tonight, as if it was irresponsible or even immoral. And then you begin to wonder if you've really seen anything. Your eyes were closed most of the time anyway, weren't they? All you really saw was blackness. There is a terrible, black void out there, and you're not sure you want to return in the morning. You would rather go back to the grocery store. The grocery store had postcards. You could buy them and send them to some of your friends who don't know what you're doing this summer, scribbling your initials at the bottom of the cards so they wonder whose handwriting it is.

Weeks later, they'll call you: "Was that you at the Grand Canyon?" they'll ask.

"Why, yes," you'll say. "I was there. I was there at that grocery store. I saw it. I bought ground beef and tomato sauce. I touched it. I felt it. I smelled it. I was there. Why are *you* being so critical of me? Why are *you* asking me all these questions. Go there yourself. Go there and then you'll be silent. You won't say a word about it."

Just as you're trying to think of an excuse to go back to the grocery store tomorrow so you can avoid going to the Rim, you hear the first clap of thunder. You see the first bolt of lightning snap over the sky in the direction of that expanse of blackness. That blackness is out there, slowly creeping toward you. What if geological time were sped up overnight by millions of years and the abyss swallowed you before dawn? It could happen, you think to yourself. Why not? Why should you feel confident that you'll live through the night? You and your Cro-magnon ancestors who have walked the Earth for only ten thousand years. Think of the trilobites. Spiny little crustacean-like creatures of the ancient seas. They ruled the world for millions of years. Millions. They were proud. They were kings, reigning over every other life form for eons. And now you can find their fossils embedded in the limestone of that Canyon. Just how long before *you're* a fossil on the Kaibab Plateau?

Another clap of thunder. Another snap of lightning out in the distance. Soon the rain is upon you, drumming against the aluminum roof of the truck. The kids are screaming, and the director of this tour, the owner of the company, is staring at you: "They could use a little support!" he says. The other counselors are already off to their respective tents, and you step into the darkness and slowly make your way to the writhing and screaming at the other end of camp, lifting up apologies to Vishnu, hoping he will not visit you tonight, praying he will not sweep you away and bury you at the bottom of the Canyon in the Vishnu Schist.

*   *   *

The morning is cold and quiet, and the director, like always, wakes you so you can wake the boys in your tent. "Hey, sun's comin' up soon. We gotta move," he says.

You awake the same way you do every morning you hear his voice—with a start and a whimper. It's a humiliating whimper, like a child's coming out of a bad dream. You quickly mumble something, you don't even know what, but it's only for the sound effect. Your voice is dry and raspy, masculine, you think. You want the sound of it to overcome the whimper your boss has just heard.

No breakfast until later this morning before you hit the road to Utah. Priority now is to get to the Rim as quick as possible. Sunrise at the Grand Canyon is an optional part of this trip for the teens. They're allowed to sleep through it if they choose, though encouraged to come along. Surprisingly, most of them do come, shuffling back and forth like the walking dead as they approach the Ryder truck. The plan is to pile everybody into the back of the truck because it will be faster than taking the bus.

You haven't come up with a good excuse not to go to the Rim. The market isn't open this early in the morning. So, you sit in the back of the truck atop the cooler where you've stored the ground beef for the lasagna, wondering if your semicircular canals will keep your balance this time, or if you'll fall to your death in front of these kids, permanently obliterating any desire that they might have had to go West later in life. Although, the more you think about it, maybe that would be best for them. Why should they be like you and keep searching for Eden? They'd be better off to stay in New Jersey and be content with what they have. They should know the truth. They should know that mountain ranges as majestic as the Himalayas and the Alps rose and vanished on the site of the Grand Canyon before life got any further than the protozoa or the jellyfish. They should know that when they turn middle-aged they will look to the young Western landscape in search of immortality, but Nature seems to regret whatever it makes, and while they gaze at their youth, Nature is already busy tearing down its creation, dissolving both man and mountain to sand and mud.

You step off the truck, wondering if the ground is really solid or if it will shift right below your feet and evaporate into dust. You can feel more light surrounding you and there is a sense of urgency to get to the Rim. The kids, still half asleep, are actually jogging. You can't bring yourself to run to the abyss, though. You already did that last night. You take your time, and when you get to the lookout point the sun is already coming up over the horizon. A light haze is hovering across the Canyon. You can see the air, as if it were fluid, and as you hold onto the wire fence separating you from a five-thousand-foot drop, you think it is the air that allows you to keep your equilibrium. You lift up more prayers and apologies to Vishnu and your confidence rises a little. You're standing on the edge. Still standing. This is progress.

Soon the sun is burning off the haze, and the director tells the kids they can roam in groups for an hour and a half. Everyone disperses and you're left there alone, clinging to the fence. Let go, you say to yourself. Let go, it'll be okay.

So, you do let go and set off in a westerly direction along the Rim, one foot in front of the other, small steps, your knees feeling just a little bit weak. But you're proud of yourself. You're recovering from last night's experience. You may go on to lead a normal life, whatever normal is. You still haven't looked down, but you're walking along the Rim of the Grand Canyon. You're there. You feel it. It really is there. It's not a grocery store.

You come to the famous trail you've seen in pictures, the one that goes all the way down, the one that the mules navigate so competently, more competently than you ever could. For a moment, you ponder stepping into the abyss and walking down the trail for a few minutes, but you're afraid the mules will get in your way and squeeze you closer to the edge. So, instead, you go onto one of the rock platforms that juts out toward the sky. Then you get down on your hands and knees and actually crawl to the brink. There's no wire fence here. You're looking straight ahead into the vast amount of space in front of you, but the space doesn't seem to be the barrier it was last night. It's thinner now; you get the feeling it won't hold you back today. What's worse is that all that space seems to be beckoning you. "Look," it says. "You must look."

The look can only be down, and you try to resist, but the shame the Canyon made you feel yesterday makes you obey. Still on your hands and knees, you lean forward, then lie flat on your belly, the morning rock cool against your body. You shimmy forward, then crane your neck over the edge of the cliff.

At first you're squinting, your eyes half closed, afraid of what you'll see, but as you open them wider you see the drop below you isn't four thousand feet, but more like four hundred to the next precipice, then another few hundred to the next plateau. Of course, you have no idea how accurate your depth perception is, but at least there isn't a sheer wall that plunges a mile down. And as you look at the different slopes and terraces below, each separated not so much by distance as by millions of years in geologic time, they become strangely familiar to you, as if you had been here before.

You begin to see rolling fields and meadows that somehow seem friendly to you. You see the Berkshires, soft, inviting hills, with church steeples rising through leaves turned the colors of autumn. And you smell those leaves rather than the pines. You breathe it in and smell the comfort of home, the leaves crunching underneath your feet as you run through them. Your legs are strong and you breathe easy, passing by brick houses with ivy creeping up their walls, rows of elm trees towering above you. You run until the sidewalk ends and the houses and automobiles are in the distance behind you. Then you slow down and enter the woods, finding the path that winds down to a stream that runs straight through a big rock that looks like it's been sliced in two. And you sit up on top of the rock and watch the water run beneath you, wondering where the stream is coming from and where it's going. You want to follow the stream and find where it empties, but you can't today because you have to be home for dinner soon. So, you make a pact with yourself that you'll do it another time, and you seal the pact by taking a piece of chalk out of your coat pocket and writing your initials and the date on the rock. Only it rains the next day and you're sure your pact has been washed away. Then the next day you have to stay after school for the sixth-grade spelling bee even though you're eliminated in the first round, and the next day you have to study for your history test on World War II to make up for the spelling bee, and the next day you have to go to dinner at your grandparents' house because you failed the history test and your mother thinks you should learn from primary sources, and the next day you're kissing Donna Delano behind the woodshed in her backyard because she knows nothing about history and spells worse than you.

Then you lose track and you can only remember special days. Like the day you graduated from junior high when your leg was broken because you fell out of a tree fooling around, trying to impress Angela Landry, but your mother still wanted you to go up on stage to receive your diploma, so you did and you tripped over your crutches and fell down the stairs in front of the entire eighth grade. Like the day you first took your road test hoping to get your driver's license and you had an asthma attack while you were trying to do your three-point turn, and the registry officer just kept yelling at you to turn the wheel while you wheezed and coughed, while all the air in the car disappeared. Like the day you missed your high school prom because your car broke down on the way to pick up your date who lived in another town, and you stood in a tuxedo on the side of a road for an hour and a half until the tow truck came with a man named Rex who just laughed at you and said you should have taken a limo, that you shouldn't have even bothered to get your driver's license. Like the day of your college graduation when you stood there among five thousand other people, soaked from the champagne bottle the guy next to you exploded in your face, feeling lonely, feeling sad that you missed your date for the high school prom four years ago and dejected because you have no one to share your academic achievement with.

And when you get home you call Donna Delano's house to see whatever happened to her, but her mother says she lives in Peoria with her husband and child. And you begin to think that time is running out for you, even though you're only twenty-two. And you put on twenty pounds in one year. And you join a health club and spend another year taking the weight off. And you'll be approaching thirty soon, but it feels more like sixty. So you quit your job as an assistant librarian at a community college and resolve to get yourself together, only you're not sure what you should do. And in the back of your mind you still remember that you never did find where that boyhood stream emptied out in the woods behind your old neighborhood. For all you know, it could be one of the Colorado's tributaries. But instead of going home to fulfill your pact, you sign on as a counselor for a teen tour and go West from New Jersey until you find yourself here, looking down into the Grand Canyon, trying to see the river, but you can't. It's hidden some place a mile below. So you resolve to go down and find it, and while you're down there you'll find the spot where the Hopis think life began, too.

But then you remember you have responsibilities. Breakfast is at nine and then the bus leaves for Utah. You're still lying there on your chest, looking down into the graveyard of history, trying to decide what to do. And then you see Vishnu rising from some place in the middle of the Canyon, pointing westward, urging you to look. So you do, and you see the river rising up from below, and you see water sweeping over the plateau, and, as it washes over you, you taste its salt, and you feel jagged pieces of broken sea shells scraping against your arms and legs, and then you see the trilobites floating in front of your nose, come back to reclaim the Earth. You start to flail about because you can't breathe, and you swim upward as best you can, pushing through the trilobites, and the shells, and the bones. And when you reach the surface you're there at the Rim of the Grand Canyon again, the sun shining down brightly, Shiva and Brahma standing tall before you. Isis, Odin, Osiris, and Horus by their side.

Sex Without Sight

I would see the blind woman going up and down Connecticut Avenue in the morning, this white lab, her seeing-eye dog, towing her along. She always dressed to the hilt. I couldn't fathom how a blind woman could have such fashion sense. Every day it was a slinky dress, or a sharp pantsuit, or one of those long skirts with flowers on it, gently blowing in the wind. And hats. She always wore hats. One day a big sun hat with a red ribbon wrapped around it, tied in a bow on the side. The next day a beret or a Boston Red Sox baseball cap. Once she even had a cowboy hat, pulled down tight over her forehead where it rested just above those dark glasses she always wore.

I'd see her a couple of times a week, either on the subway platform or out on the street. I'd watch her from a distance, and once in a while I'd walk by and stare at her legs or stare right into her dark glasses. She never seemed to register my presence, but how would I know? This went on for weeks. I got a little obsessive over it, I admit. I'd start looking for her right after I left my apartment in the morning and then again on the way home. If a week went by where I didn't see her, I felt a little disappointed and lonely.

I was a little uptight, anyway. I hadn't been sleeping much. My doctor said it was all in my head, which I emphatically denied. I wasn't making anything up. Many times I'd only sleep three hours a night. It wasn't enough. Sometimes I'd be lying there still awake when the trash trucks came down the alley and my upstairs neighbor got into the shower. Sometimes on weekends I'd booze enough to make myself pass out and get in a restless eight or nine hours. The doc told me to get some exercise and he gave me some pills to help me sleep. I did try getting some more exercise, but most of it consisted of long walks around my neighborhood, looking for the blind woman, searching, trying to guess where she might live. I never took those sleeping pills, though. Booze on a Friday night was one thing, drugs were another. I didn't want to become dependent on anything.

On these sleepless nights, I watched the late, late night news. I felt I had a bond with the news anchors at this hour. It's as if they were giving the news personally to me. I know it's not true, but in the middle of the night on a Tuesday you feel like you're the only one up watching TV. Sometimes the news anchors exhibit a certain amount of humor at that hour. They make these dry quips and jokes, which you never see them do on the prime-time news with Tom Brokaw. You get to the point where you start to feel like the anchors are picking the stories just for you, like you need to hear about this story because it's going to change your life. And my story, undoubtedly, was the one about the rich guy who decided he wanted to be the first person to circle the world in a hot air balloon.

It was 3:30 in the morning when they cut live to him and his balloon in some stadium in St. Louis. An interviewer on site relayed a question from the anchor and the balloon man responded, saying, "The winds are good. We're going to give it a go." He looked right into the camera. "There's no time like the present, Hal. We make history tonight."

The video cut back to the anchor and I swear he said: "We are coming to you live from St. Louis where a rich guy is about to embark on man's last great aviation journey. He will attempt to circumnavigate the globe in a hot air balloon. Our thoughts and prayers are with him. We can only hope this will pick up our ratings as he battles thunderstorms, freezing temperatures, and our insomniac viewers' limited attention span."

Back in the stadium, there was a whoosh of gas, a flame lit up the sky, and then the balloon slowly drifted up into the darkness. It was an awesome sight. There was this rich guy floating up into the air, waving to his friends and support team down below on the turf.

"Hal, the theme from the movie *Rocky*, 'Gonna Fly Now,' is blaring over the loudspeaker here," the reporter in the stadium said to the anchor. "Clearly, this man is on a mission."

"Only time will tell if we are witnessing history tonight," the anchor said. "Off into the night goes a man of courage, brave enough to cross the oceans and the continents with nothing but his wits, his helium, and twenty-five million dollars to finance such an expedition. We wish him Godspeed."

Evidently, the balloon man had made a fortune in commodities or something like that, and now he was looking for a way to leave his mark on the world by doing something no one else had ever done. I admit, there was something to that for me. There was something to how he stood there on the stadium field and said, "There's no time like the present, Hal. We make history tonight." He said it with such authority. He was a man of conviction. One had to admire that. A man with conviction must sleep well at night. Besides, everybody loves a rich guy with a plan to buck the odds, especially if there's great peril involved. It's the American way. Send that rich guy up there in a balloon, over an ocean. See if he comes back. If he does, we'll make a hero out of him and he can have all the babes he wants.

I was pretty excited the day the balloon man launched. For some reason, it renewed my vigor for finding the blind woman. In the morning, I let two or three trains pass by on the subway, hoping her and her dog would show up on the platform. I hit the streets hard after work in search of her. I combed through grocery stores, peeked in coffee shops, even got on a bus once, just in case she'd moved to ground transportation. Everywhere I went I searched the newspaper racks for glimmers of news about the balloon man. Buried on page fourteen of one paper was a picture of him standing next to his balloon giving the thumbs-up sign. He wore a body suit, a helmet, and dark sunglasses. He looked like a smiling space alien. You'd have to figure he'd have trouble if he went down in some remote African village. The natives wouldn't know what to make of him.

I started to fear the blind woman left town; I hadn't seen her for two weeks. People are like that here in Washington. Here today, gone tomorrow. Not me, though. I've put in almost seven years at the Department of Transportation. You don't just walk away from that—you take the subway or high-speed rail! That's the joke around the office, anyway. Truth be told, I actually was pretty idealistic when I started working there. There's always been something with me and motion. I have to be moving, or I have to watch things that are moving. I like cars, I like planes, trains too. I used to run a lot. There's nothing like the feeling of running down a hill, your arms spread, feeling the air rushing past you and your heart pumping, your legs pounding. It's almost like sex.

Transportation seemed like the logical place for me to end up (I started off at Interior, but didn't last more than two years there). I was ambitious in the beginning. I hoped I'd move up in the ranks. I spent my time thinking of ways to try to improve the flow of traffic on U.S. interstates. I wrote memos to my superiors about my ideas. My non-government friends teased me about it, saying I was a glorified pot-hole filler. But really, when I was bright-eyed about it, the job was about removing clutter and getting people moving again. It was about getting people to use public transit, lesser-used roads, new roads, hot air balloons—anything to beat the gridlock. I haven't had many successes at DOT, though. I did once work on a multibillion-dollar plan for a commuter rail system in Cleveland, but it never made it past the city council. After that debacle, things kind of went downhill. It was like I missed my stop and couldn't get off the train. I just kept riding along, year in, year out, building up my government pension. Eventually, I even stopped running. I didn't start walking a lot again until I was out looking for the blind woman.

After not seeing her for so long, I was about to give up when I saw her on a Saturday—right after the balloon man had successfully crossed the Atlantic. She was walking with the dog by the zoo. I nearly froze in my tracks and stood there with my newspaper and half gallon of milk hanging by my side. She was wearing short-shorts and a tank-top T-shirt, with a Boston Bruins cap flipped around backwards on her head. A total knockout. She had the body of an athlete. I mean, she had runners legs and these shiny, sculpted arms, tanned just right—not skin-cancer tanned, just enough color to make them glow in the sunlight.

She was waiting for the light to change so she could cross the street and I looked her over good. I mean, why not? It was free, right? She'd never know I was looking at her. She bent over to pat the dog and her shorts rode up. You could see part of her behind. I got a nice view. Other guys were looking, too. She turned heads.

I followed her across the street and kept a few feet behind her, trying to figure out what to do. I didn't have a plan for this moment, but I felt the need to say something to her, even to ask her out. The balloon man had just crossed the Atlantic. I needed my own achievement for the day.

I walked along side of her for about two blocks, trying to think of something—anything— to say. I'm not good with women. I generally don't know what to do with them. All I could think to comment on was the weather. It'd been raining for a couple of days, but there was sunshine now, drying out the street. It was getting steamy and humid. Her dog looked hot and panting. But how stupid would that be? "Your dog looks hot. Can I give him some water?" Ridiculous. I don't know why relationships between the sexes have to be so complicated. Why can't we just tell each other what's on our minds? And then it hit me. If honesty was the cornerstone of any relationship, I would start with that and tell her what I was thinking.

I walked up beside her, crinkling my grocery bag and jingling my keys so she would know I was there. Then I went for it.

"Did you hear about that rich guy who's trying to go around the world in a hot air balloon?"

She turned her head toward me, as if she wasn't certain if I were talking to her. She didn't slow her pace at all, the dog leading her a long.

"I heard he made it across the Atlantic," she said, her words, her fabulous words, spoken not necessarily to me, but out into the world, loudly and proudly, for all to hear that she, too, had heard of the rich guy in the balloon. I felt an instant bond and identification with her and I knew I would like her.

"Yeah, yeah, the guy's right on schedule," I said. "This could be a big event if he makes it. This could be history."

"I've ridden in a hot air balloon," she said. "You feel weightless. You're swept away by the wind and the air is light and cool, and you gasp sometimes because you hit air bumps and you free-fall for a few feet at a time. It's exhilarating."

"I'd like to try it sometime."

"There's a place in Virginia that sails balloons. You can take a ride there. I have the information somewhere at home."

This was truly destiny. For a second, I was glad she was blind because I could feel my face turning red and I was smiling ear to ear. We talked for a little while longer, then I asked for her number so I could get information about the ballooning place in Virginia. I memorized the digits, ran home and lifted up a prayer of thanks to the balloon man for giving me the inspiration.

I called her later that day and we talked for well over an hour. Her name was Claire and she'd been blind since she was twelve. I don't know what caused her blindness; she didn't get into it. But apparently the lights were completely out. She could sense movement, but she couldn't see shadows or anything. Still, she'd gone on and gotten a degree in music. She played the viola. Once she even played for a symphony, and now she worked with blind kids in a program where they learned about music. It was pretty damn admirable. More admirable than anything I've ever done.

She was from Newton, Massachusetts, where both her parents were dentists. She'd never had a cavity in her life and said that was one of the perks of being blind—you had fewer other ailments because you had one big one that took up most of your time. Her dog's name was Blister. Her favorite food was cheese. She ran on a treadmill for forty-five minutes a day. She said she thought she was fat in her early twenties, but she wasn't sure. Her favorite book was *The Devils* by Dostoyevsky, which is over fourteen hundred pages long in Braille. As a kid she wanted to be a fireman. She'd once smoked dope on the steps of the U.S. Capitol. Most Saturday nights she stayed home and listened to classical music or reggae.

We made plans to meet for coffee the next day.

The balloon man's mission control center is comprised of top-flight engineers, meteorologists, and volunteer well-wishers. They monitor his every movement around the clock. They even know when he defecates. Seriously. They're worried about his health and monitor it carefully. "Successful bowel movement at nineteen hundred hours!" Mission control cheers. The balloon man is regular. He eats military-style MREs—Meals Ready to Eat—which are loaded with the nutrients and fiber he needs. His latrine is a bucket.

His one indulgence is coffee—a Swiss-mocha blend that comes in packets. He admits it's not real coffee, but it's probably better than the java me and the blind woman have at the shop up the street. For $3.50 a cup, you'd think there was opium or cocaine in it. I tried to pay, but the blind woman, Claire, insisted on going Dutch. She had had a long day. Her ex-boyfriend from two years ago called her. He, too, is blind, and he has decided to marry another blind woman, someone Claire has not heard of until now.

"He wants my blessing," she said to me in the coffee shop. "For what? 'You don't need me for validation anymore, Steven,' I told him. 'You stopped needing me a long time ago. You just go back to your sweet little new woman and live happily ever after. I don't give a fuck what you do!'"

She used to live with this blind man. She was involved with him for three years and then one day he woke up and said he was unsatisfied with his life and that he had to move on. He said this to her on a Sunday morning and they fought for the next three days. The Wednesday following Claire came home from work and he was in their apartment with another woman—the "floozy, the fling," Claire called her—a different woman than the one he was planning to marry now. The two of them were sitting on the couch smoking cigarettes. The other woman was not blind.

"It was the only time I really wished I could still see," Claire said, sipping her coffee. "I wished I'd had a gun, too, so I could have blown his brains out. Now he wants me to go to his wedding to another woman. He just wants to be alleviated of his guilt. I won't give him the satisfaction."

She was distraught. Her hands were shaking. Coffee wasn't a good idea. "I'm sorry, but can we just get out of here?" she said. "I have that balloon information back at my place, but your eyes would help me find it a lot more quickly. Are you trustworthy or are you some kind of freak? Can I let you into my place to give you this information?"

I didn't know how to respond to that. I suppose it would be easy to take advantage of a blind woman—she had to be careful. She didn't wait for me to answer, though. We blew the coffee joint and handed seven dollars worth of coffee to a homeless guy outside. He thanked us profusely as we left. He had no teeth.

She calmed down during the short walk to her place. It was a cool spring evening now, the sun just going down. She folded her arms across her chest and I could see goose pimples rising up off her skin. She only wore a short-sleeve button-down shirt and shorts. As we went around a corner I caught a guy looking her over, staring at her butt. I gave him a menacing look. That sort of thing irked me now because she was clearly with me. And I admit, I started to feel a little ashamed about how I looked at her the day before and the other times I'd seen her on the street.

I wondered how many guys looked at her in that way every day. I started to think I needed to look at women a little more judiciously. I started to think that every woman only has so many stares to give. I mean, she'll have thousands, but maybe each look takes something away from her. And each leer takes even more. It sucks something right out of them. It hastens aging and it keeps going until there are no looks left to give, and by this time a woman is categorized in the elder category: she's a grandmother, or she's an "ant" (which is an elder aunt), she's a diplomat, or the secretary of Health and Human Services, and so on and so forth.

We got to her street. Claire stretched her arms into the air and said, "I wish I could fly. It's a silly wish, I know, but no sillier than wishing I could see. I like winged things. They have more freedom than you and I will ever know."

She lived in a big attic with a private entrance, which she rented from an old woman on Davenport. As we entered, she left the dog, Blister, downstairs. But she had this down pat—she went right up the stairs and around the landing, her shoes clomping loudly against the old wood. She pulled the string to a light that was bolted onto the wall and I figured that was for my benefit, but then again I wasn't sure. I'd never been in a blind person's apartment. I'd only seen them in the movies and in the movies they didn't sit there in the dark. But I supposed they could because I remembered this one picture about a blind woman who was being stalked by some killer in her house. She got away after a thunderstorm knocked the power out and she bashed him over the head with a frying pan. The killer, he never saw it coming without the lights on, but it didn't seem to make any difference to the blind woman.

Claire's apartment was pretty Spartan, as one might imagine. It was a big efficiency with a bed in the corner and a small kitchen on the opposite end. There was a tapestry hanging on one wall with a picture of a globe and the words THE GOOD EARTH in raised lettering. On the coffee table there was this knickknack—a pink flamingo with a weight underneath its feet. I gave it a start with my finger and the flamingo magically kept bobbing back and forth as if there were some supernatural force at work in her apartment. All of her hats were piled on a bookshelf, which also had a picture of Blister and her, standing at attention by a mailbox. There was a carton of spilled dog biscuits on the floor. Her viola sat on a stand in the corner of the apartment.

"Come," she said, and she led me by the hand to a bureau on the other side of the room. She pulled open the top drawer and said, "There's a flyer for the balloon company somewhere in here."

I rummaged through the dresser. It was loaded with crap. There was unopened mail. There was a Braille Bible. There were pictures of her and her blind boyfriend—which I found extremely odd. They were standing out in a field somewhere, dressed in bathing suits. In one shot he was holding his walking cane. In the next, he had a Frisbee. In the next, Claire was putting an inordinate amount of sunscreen on his hairy chest. All of the pictures were off-centered, some of them with half of their bodies cut off, as if they were taken by another blind person who didn't know exactly where to aim the camera. But what would blind people be doing with a camera and pictures anyway? There was also a deck of cards in the drawer, videotapes, a calculator, two watches, a thermometer. I didn't know what she did with any of this stuff. There were prophylactics. Then, buried underneath a book on airplanes, was the information on "Greico's Heavenly Balloon Rides . . . *departing four times daily for the other side of paradise.*" The flyer had pictures of attractive couples, smiling with big white teeth as if their breath had just been taken away. It was a real romantic scene.

"I found it," I said. "Maybe we can go sometime." I shoved the flyer into my back pocket.

"I'd probably like that," she said.

She had been sitting on the love seat in the middle of the room while I was looking for the balloon stuff. She had brushed out her hair and stretched out her long, shiny legs across the coffee table. She looked extremely hip. With her dark glasses on she looked like a New York socialite or something. She looked like she was attending a fashion show and I half-expected her to order me to walk back and forth in front of her in some kind of bizarre runway game. But she just turned her head toward me as if she were looking right at me and patted the cushion beside her with her hand.

"Charles, sit here," she said. That's my name, but nobody calls me Charles. Charlie, maybe. But usually I just go by Chuck. I liked it when she said *Charles*, though. For a second I actually felt sophisticated.

She was real quiet for a while, her foot bobbing up and down at the end of her leg like the flamingo on the coffee table. I started to feel a little on edge, especially after seeing the prophylactics in the drawer. I wasn't sure what to expect. But I kept looking at her legs and I started to fantasize. I began to rethink my theory on lust and how many *looks* a woman had to give. I wondered about women who are involved in porn or *Playboy* or those other mags with nude women in them that men look at all the time. I wondered if women who participate in such things have all that much more taken away from them. Someone should do a study on retired women who were once centerfolds to see if they look older or more used up than their counterparts who did not. Still, I thought, there's got to be a difference between a woman posing in a mag and a blind woman on the street.

Finally, Claire said, "Come closer, Charles." She sounded like my fifth-grade teacher, Mrs. Lipson, who I secretly had a crush on and always obeyed without hesitation. So, I slid on over until my leg was touching hers. She looked at me, or at least faced me, as if she were about to kiss me. I could feel that rush of excitement I always get when I kiss a new woman, and just as I thought it was going to happen, she reached over and grabbed something off the end table. Then I heard a click and all of a sudden this electric buzzing sound filled the room. She had something in her hand, and as she moved it closer to me I really began to get nervous because it sounded like one of those sex toys or something, and I like to fool around, but I'm really kind of a traditional guy when it comes down to it.

She grabbed me from the back of my head and shoved this object right in front of my face. I started to panic, wondering what the hell I'd gotten myself into. But then she started to glide it gently over my scalp and I realized it was just some cockamamie brush with batteries in it. It vibrated like crazy when she ran it through my hair. It was a little disconcerting, but it felt good. She ran the brush over my head with her right hand and then smoothed my hair down with her left. The whole thing felt great. I would have been ready to fall asleep if it weren't so erotic. She went at this for a while, until finally I whispered in her ear, "You want me to brush your hair now?"

Her face got all aglow when I said that. She smiled and said softly, "You want to brush my hair? Steven never brushed *my* hair."

I took the brush from her and she took her glasses off. Her eyes were closed. I spent a good fifteen minutes working on her hair; it was so thick and soft and it smelled pretty, like she used expensive shampoo. She kept her eyes closed the whole time, but her face lit up with this steady smile. After a little while, she took the brush out of my hand and put it back on the end table.

"Thank you," she said. "That was lovely."

Then there was a long, awkward silence between us. We both sat on the couch, not touching each other, facing straight ahead. She took soft, quiet breaths that sped up a little. Without any warning, she began to unbutton her shirt, slowly, one button at a time, still facing straight ahead in the direction of the pink flamingo. Once she finished, she slipped the shirt off her shoulders and sat there quietly in her bra. I was trying not stare, but then, what the heck, she was coming on to me. So, I take a good look and my heart beat a little faster. She was in such excellent shape. I could see ripples in her stomach. I could only be thankful she wouldn't be able to see I'd been letting myself go lately. I'd been telling myself I could go back to the gym any day, sort of like a smoker or a drug addict tells himself he can quit any time he wants. There'd been a couple of times I even planned to start the workout regime again. Run my three miles, stair climb for twenty minutes, curls, crunches, bench presses—the whole nine yards to fitness. I used to do it all. But lately, more and more I'd just been too tired. I couldn't quite seem to get on track.

There was a short, round candle on the table, melted down in an ashtray, with some matches beside it. I lit the candle, trying to set the mood—for myself, I suppose. I wondered what a blind woman was doing with matches and a candle and if it was a safe idea.

"What are you doing?" she said, still not moving.

"I just lit the candle," I said. "A little ambiance."

"They smell nice," she said. "This one is lilac. I love the smell of flowers."

I put my arm around her and cuddled up a little closer to her. There was a draft coming from somewhere. The candle flickered on the table. I wondered if she was cold, sitting there with no shirt on. I looked around for a blanket but didn't see one. I began to caress the back of her neck.

She faced me, her eyes rolling back and forth as if they were trying to focus in on something. They were hazel-colored. For a second she seemed to look right at me, but then it was lost and her eyes rolled back into her head. This, I admit, gave me a pause.

She leaned in closer. I thought she was going to kiss me, but I didn't feel ready. I wished she'd put the glasses back on. I backed off a little.

"I need you to tell me something," she said. She took a deep breath and her chest heaved up and down.

"What is it?" I said, starting to think she wanted to know how her breasts looked. I mean, that would be conceivable, wouldn't it? A blind woman might have never seen her breasts. She might have wanted to know if they were attractive. And believe me, they were something. I was trying to think of a way to describe them to her without using a cliché like "melon" or "handful" when she started talking again.

"Look at it and tell me what you think," she said. "On my back, below my shoulder. There's a tattoo. A butterfly. It's a *blue morpho*. My beautiful *blue morpho*."

This was getting more erotic than I ever imagined. I had never made it with a woman who had a tattoo, or with a blind woman for that matter. She closed her eyes and leaned forward into my lap, holding her breasts in her arms. I couldn't have been more aroused.

But as she nestled her head in my lap, the titillation was replaced by anxiety. There was a tattoo all right. But it was no beautiful blue butterfly. It was a dirty-green sea horse with flames and smoke coming out of its nostrils.

"How long have you had this?" I asked her.

"Five years," she said. "I showed the tattoo artist a picture from a book I've had since I was a little a girl, when I was be able to see. I used to have twenty-twenty. I used to be quick enough to catch butterflies in a net. My father and I would go up to the mountains and we'd lie in meadows and catch them all day. And I know it wasn't. I'm positive it wasn't. But for some reason, I keep remembering that *blue morpho* as the last thing I ever saw."

She buried her head in my lap and wrapped her arms around me. "Is it beautiful?" she asked. "Is the tattoo beautiful?"

The tattoo was the most heinous thing I'd ever seen. It was an evil-looking, flame-snorting sea horse. It was one of the most vile things I'd ever seen in my life.

I lied. "Yes, it's really pretty. Just like you."

I felt my face getting flush and I wondered if it was a trick and she was going to tell me she knew I was lying to her. But nothing. She nestled down in my lap. I became very uncomfortable. I had just lied to a blind woman—and it was a big lie. This wasn't getting our relationship off to the right start.

She ran her hands up underneath my shirt and caressed my chest hair.

"It's been a long time since I've been with someone," she said, and then she pressed her lips against my belly. She took my shirt off and kissed me all over my chest, my shoulders, and my arms. She was a kissing fiend. Non-stop, one right after the other. They were small kisses, but pleasant. She made a little puckering sound each time she planted one on me. It was the sweetest thing I ever heard. Then she planted one right on my lips. I mean, it was a direct hit. You might think a blind woman would fumble about for a while, but she seemed to know exactly where all the merchandise was. Once she slipped me the tongue, I couldn't take it anymore. This was going to go too far. I couldn't get the tattoo out of mind. I couldn't have dishonest sex with a blind woman.

She started nibbling on my ear, driving me wild. But I couldn't go through with it. I was caressing her back right where the tattoo was. I had to tell her the truth, but there were big ramifications. I don't just mean the mood would have been ruined. How do you tell someone her body has been defaced and, even worse, she hasn't known about it for years? She'd never be able to trust a tattooist again. Once she started reaching for my pants, that was it. I flung her off of me and shot up like I'd just sat on a nail. I tripped on the coffee table and knocked over the bobbing flamingo.

"What?" she said. "What is it?"

"Nothing," I said as I righted the flamingo and blew out the candle. "It's not you, it's me. It's totally me. I just can't."

"Why? Don't you find me attractive?"

"I find you extremely attractive. More than you'll ever know. But I have to go. I'm sorry."

I kissed her on the forehead, threw my shirt back on, and made my way to the stairs. "Charles?" she said. She still sat there on the couch, topless, and utterly confused. "Charles?" I heard her say again as I went to the door, the dog watching me on my way out.

*   *   *

The balloon man lives in a box that's six feet by four feet. He travels 40 to 50 miles per hour at an altitude of about 24,000 feet above sea level. He breathes from liquid oxygen cylinders much of the time and sleeps only two hours a night. It's below freezing most of the way. He wears two pairs of wool socks and expensive waterproof boots from L.L. Bean, but his feet are always cold, or numb. He walks in place, trying to shake the pins and needles that plague him. He fiddles with his heater, which hasn't been working properly since the second day of his journey. Mission control worries more about the heater than his fuel reserves, which are lower than expected.

I worry, too. I'd rather see him go crashing down in a village in Pakistan, out of fuel, but desperately trying to go another mile or two, than see him have to pack it in because his feet are cold. Not that frostbite isn't a legitimate concern, but I'd like to think that the balloon man is better than the elements. You are no longer human when you're floating at 24,000 feet. You're closer to God up there. If he makes it back to St. Louis, I picture him climbing out of the balloon looking like Moses after he's just come down from Mt. Sinai—his hair's completely white, he's got a beard, and he looks like he's aged some thirty years but with that he's gained a thousand years of wisdom.

I could have used some wisdom on Monday. I did not see Claire. In fact, I was on the lookout for her on my way to work and would have avoided her if I did see her—not that that would have been very hard to do. I didn't know what to say to her. No excuse I could come up with sounded legitimate. I was afraid she would think I wasn't interested because she was blind, which was hardly the case.

By 5:00 p.m. I was depressed. I got home hoping there would be good news from the skies over Africa later that night, but at 2:30 a.m. my anchor person said, "The situation is dire." Apparently, the Libyans vowed to shoot my balloonist down if he tried to cross their air space. But an alternate route would expend too much fuel and threaten the completion of the journey altogether.

"This worldwide balloon voyage is at a crisis point," the news anchor said. "Will our sky commander risk death at the hands of Colonel Khaddhafi, who has drawn a line in the sky and ordered him not to cross? Or will our fearless flyer burn the extra precious fuel to cross Africa through an alternate route?"

Mission control was frantic. They had feared this and their search for moderate diplomatic channels had failed. My man in the balloon was suddenly in the throes of an international crisis. He floated peacefully somewhere above the Mediterranean, while below him a head of state was threatening to blow him out of the sky. There were reports from Washington. The State Department did not want to get involved. They had warned mission control to stay clear of Libya and various other hostile countries. They urged him to turn back. The bureaucrats! Couldn't they see that the stakes were high? To the Beltway insiders, he may have just been a rich guy in a balloon, but to me he was a freedom fighter. He stood for all that America stood for, and now, at over 20,000 feet, he defied a dictator. Whether he completed his mission or was blown to bits, he took a stand and he was leaving his mark on the world. He wasn't going to run from anyone.

I couldn't say the same for myself. I'd just run out on a beautiful woman who wanted to make love to me. The whole prospect of it was asinine. If I were an adventurer like the balloon man, I would have thrown caution to the wind and swept her off her feet, flaring-nostriled sea horse or not. Now I was alone and pining away for her, afraid to even call her. I tried to sleep but it was a lost cause. I kept thinking of the silky, smooth skin on Claire's back surrounding her tattoo. I imagined what she would look like naked. I imagined driving through the countryside with her, going on romantic picnics and paddle boat rides, enjoying wine tastings and apple picking. But every fantasy ended with us in bed and me freezing at the site of the tattoo.

I wasn't sure what the balloon man would do under the same circumstances, but I knew that unlike me he'd do something. He was a man of action. He'd probably search the countryside for a blue morpho butterfly and present it to the blind woman as a token of his affections and an apology. "This is the butterfly you were seeking when you got that tattoo, my dear. And this is the real thing," he'd say. Of course, she'd have no way of verifying if it were a real blue morpho, but she'd believe a rich guy with his own hot air balloon. He was a man of honesty and integrity. I couldn't exactly say the same for myself.

I wanted to call Claire and tell her the balloon man was on the verge of becoming an international incident—albeit one that was scattered all over the Mediterranean. Mission control had lost contact with him right at the critical juncture and I was really on edge. I knew Claire would be sympathetic, but I also knew she'd want to know why I bolted on Saturday night. I paced around my apartment hoping there'd be another news report on my man's condition, but there was nothing. By early morning, I had to get some air, so I went out and started doing circles around the neighborhood. I walked by Claire's place three times, hoping to see her on the way to the subway, but nothing. I showed up for work half an hour late, unshaven and unshowered. I searched for Claire and her dog on the subway on the way home, but I didn't see her tracks anywhere. I walked up and down the avenue a couple of times, but still nothing. I went home and fell asleep, fearful that the balloon man was dead. I made up my mind that if I found out he was alive later I would call Claire.

I awoke a little after 3:00 in the morning, just in time to see a clip of a jubilant mission control on TV. He'd made it by Libya. They'd left him alone. The anchorman was questioning the reporter on site: "What's the mood there? Do they feel like they can go all the way now?"

"Hal, everyone here is ecstatic," the reporter responded. "Not only are they grateful that he is alive and well, but they think they've just made it through their greatest hurdle. All systems are go and they think he can make it all the way."

I picked up the phone and dialed Claire's number before I lost my nerve.

"It's three in the morning," she said. "Are you some kind of weirdo?"

Maybe I was. I was calling a blind woman in the middle of the night to tell her that a rich guy in a balloon had escaped being shot down by a madman dictator in Africa.

"This guy in the balloon," I said. "He's made it by Libya."

"I know. I heard it on TV."

The fact that she was still following this story sent my heart palpitating. Clearly, we were very much alike. I wanted to run over to her place right then and there. I imagined us both suffering from insomnia for the rest of the week, sitting in her bed eating spaghetti while we watched the balloonist's story unfold.

I was about to apologize for leaving in such a huff the other night and ask her if I could see her again. But before I could do that she said, "Steven is here. I can't talk now."

Now, there is jealousy and then there is *jealousy*. The thought of this blind guy coming over to her place for one last blind fling before he got married—well, it was an outrage. Or even worse, what if he'd called off his wedding to start things up with Claire again? I guess I had no basis for any of this, but he was there in the middle of the night, wasn't he? What else would he be there for?

The image of them having sex was an ugly one for me. Somebody's got to be able to see, don't they? What is it like to make love to someone you can't see? Did they know what sex looked like? You have to be able to see the motion of sex for it to be satisfying, don't you? And what a waste. Claire had the most gorgeous body I'd ever seen. And this poor chump didn't even know what it looked like. I imagine he could feel her curves and her muscles and all, but it couldn't be the same. It'd be like eating strawberries when all you could do was smell them. He'd have no idea what her luscious face looked like, or how she pursed her lips or smiled when he touched her. He couldn't know the color of her hair or the arch of her back or the nape of her neck. Short-shorts and lingerie would mean nothing to him. Then again, neither would the snarling sea horse on her back. I imagined him running his lips over it time and time again, not even knowing it was there. The prospect of this frightened me. The whole prospect of sex without sight frightened me. What if it was better? They say blind people make better use of their other senses. What if the same thing applied to sex because they weren't so preoccupied with how things looked?

If that was the case, I was dead in the water. I couldn't compete.

By dawn, I'd worked myself up into a frenzy. I couldn't get the images of Claire and this guy out of my head. I imagined them going at it right there on the couch in their own blind, inept or magnificent way, bobbing up and down like the stupid pink flamingo on the coffee table. I saw them tripping over themselves as they tried to make their way to the bed, him fumbling with a prophylactic, Claire getting into position as she waited for him.

I couldn't stand it. I went out for a walk, and I know it's wrong, I know it's a little obsessive, but I found myself out in front of Claire's apartment. It wasn't like I was going to try to peak inside or anything. She didn't live on the ground floor and the lights were off anyway. I hoped my theory about blind people never turning the lights on because they don't need them was true—otherwise, this was a sure sign that they were in bed.

It was still mostly dark out, with the sun just barely starting to come up on the other side of the city. The birds were chirping like they always do at this time of day. It's my surefire way of knowing when I've had another sleepless night. But being outside, breathing in the fresh air was better than staring up at the ceiling feeling guilty for not sleeping again. So what if I was out in front of Claire's apartment? It's a free country. I wasn't in Libya or anything. No dictator was going to keep me indoors from dusk until dawn. Besides, it's no crime to be pacing on the sidewalk in front of your love interest's apartment, or even to duck behind the bushes when she comes outside with her ex-boyfriend who has just spent the night with her even as he's about to marry someone else.

At least that's what I was thinking as I peered over those shrubs and saw Claire kiss Steven on the cheek and hug him goodbye. I watched her go inside and lock the door behind her. She was wearing boxer shorts and a tank-top that showed off her chest really nicely—something that only I, not Steven could appreciate, no matter how good his intuitive blind passion might be in bed. He wore dark glasses and carried a walking stick that he tapped on the sidewalk as he came toward me. I crouched down even lower, then stood up, wondering what I was afraid of. He walked right past me on his way off of Davenport to Connecticut, tapping all along the way. I had half a mind to knock on Claire's door, but I figured she'd find that entirely too freaky. So, I followed the blind guy at a safe distance behind him.

He was a tall guy, taller than me, and he looked like he was in better shape than me. I wondered if Claire could tell the difference when she touched the both of us. I wondered if it was important to her and I resolved to start going to the gym again. Like Claire, this Steven was a pretty snappy dresser for a blind person. He wore khakis and new wing-tipped shoes that clicked on the sidewalk along with his cane.

He walked quickly for a blind guy and I picked up my pace to keep up. I guess it was easier for him to walk fast at this time of day, when there were so few people on the street. A couple of early birds passed us on their way to work. Then a sweet-looking babe jogged by us, disgustingly fit and perky for this time in the morning, and I did a double-take to check out her backside as she ran by. Steven didn't flinch. And that, I realized, was the difference between us. I'd just sucked some of the beauty out of her with a prolonged leer, and him—nothing. He just kept walking on his way. Maybe that was why Claire wanted to be with him. He didn't steal anything from her. He didn't pull any life out of her.

Claire told me that he had been blind since birth. The more I got to thinking about that, the more I thought it was an unfair advantage. I mean, the guy has never been able to look at a woman in that certain way— the double-take you do when you notice a woman's shirt is extra tight, or when you notice that her calves are extra firm with that extra bit of muscle that can bring you to your knees—well, that is, if you're a calf man like me. A calf man. It sounds like I worship the golden calf the Israelites fabricated before Moses came down and slammed the Ten Commandments on them, burying them in a heap of fire and sucking them down into the center of earth. I've never been one to worry about God's retribution, but I bet Moses would have been heaving those commandments directly at me. Something carved on the side of Mt. Sinai probably said, "Thou shalt not covet thy neighbor's blind woman."

I haven't studied the Bible much, but I do know that at one point Saul gouged his eyes out because it was his eyes that led him to sin. Without his eyes he overcame his weaknesses and became a stronger man in his handicap. I think Jesus restored his sight later on and he went on to become St. Paul. That was pretty lucky, if you asked me. If I knew I could be redeemed, I'd think about doing something radical like that. But I guess that's the point—redemption isn't guaranteed. If it were, it'd be too easy.

If there was a path to redemption, though, Steven was probably on it. After all, how could you lust if you couldn't see? Imagine, he'd gone through his whole life without a single gaze at a woman that hung just a little too long. No stiff necks for this guy. No near automobile crashes because he was looking at something he shouldn't have been looking at instead of keeping his eyes on the road. It had to be a better way of life. The constant search for body parts can be taxing, after all. The eyes wander on their own, gazing at a thigh here, an arm there, a set of lips, a slender hand, a tanned foot, and God forbid any midriff that's out in the open. Steven had no part in it; but he had Claire, or so it seemed. He was a lucky man.

I caught up to him to him and walked beside him for almost a block, his cane tapping the whole time. I edged closer and closer to him until the cane hit my foot.

"Very sorry," he said, moving away from my path. His voice was thick and deep, another gift to make up for his so-called handicap.

"Yeah, you'd just better watch it next time," I said, sounding completely ridiculous, as if there would be a next time, as if I were the evilest man in the world, telling a blind man to stay out of my way. I didn't care, though. I couldn't help myself. How conniving of him to make Claire feel safe just because he couldn't see her—if that was indeed the case. After all, he did cheat on her with some cigarette-smoking woman.

He headed for the subway, and I headed home for a shower and some caffeine.

*　　　　　*　　　　　*

Looking down on earth from 20,000 feet in an open-air box the size of a closet, the balloon man is in a position to be the world's most profound voyeur. What else can you do up there besides look down? You'd have to look down at the world before you and watch for hours on end. I know I would. You'd see it all—love, hate, reconciliation, jealousy, loneliness, fascism, democracy, bureaucracy, hypocrisy, kindness, violence, death, birth, lust, sex. From 20,000 feet it might not look like much, but you know it's down there—all of it. The body human, churning and lurching this way and that way, tripping all over itself as it does its best to propagate and proliferate into one big, sticky mess. I bet you could feel the movement of the earth from that balloon. I bet it called out to you up there. I bet it was loud as hell.

Does a man have any revelations as he's flying through the stratosphere? Does he see that he is a part of something grander than even he imagined? Or is that knowledge too much to bear? Does he have to break the world down into parts to comprehend it? What does he think about? His friends, his family, his role in the cosmos? Or does his attention span drift like the balloon, giving in to his most base and basic desires? How would you survive the struggle?

Would you dream of women? You would think there would be plenty of women waiting for you at mission control when you finally touched down in triumph, after you've gone around the globe—if you made it, that is, if you didn't go down in the middle of an ocean and get eaten by sharks. Would you anticipate that moment? Is that how you'd make it through the freezing temperatures and the uncooperative winds—by fantasizing about the babe who wrapped her arms around you as you stepped out of that box for the first time in weeks? Would you fantasize about what she'd look like? Would you think about what sex would be like your first time back on earth? It'd be different no doubt. You would have gone to Sinai and back. Everything would be different now.

Those were my thoughts over the next several days—days in which I didn't hear from Claire or see her on the street or in the subway. I pictured the balloon man looking down on all of us from up there and I felt a little naked, a little exposed, as if he could see all of my faults better than I could. I couldn't help but think that he was a far better man than me, that he never would have been as cowardly as I had been, following a blind man around like I had only to size him up and then go home with my tail between my legs. The balloon man would have grabbed him by the collar and said, "Stay away from Claire, you blind buffoon! If you think you can hurt her again, you'll wish you could watch your back because I'll be right behind you every step of the way." The balloon man was a protector and a champion. I was a government bureaucrat and a failure. But as he floated through the sky on his noble quest, he gave me hope that one day I, too, could devote my life and a third of my capital assets to a cause that would enrich the entire world. And if that turned out not to be possible, then I just hoped for one more chance with Claire.

I slept little as the days passed, taking only naps here and there. When it finally looked like I was going to get a decent night's sleep, the phone woke me up at about 3:00 in the morning. My apartment was dark and quiet, and I was disoriented, enjoying the most productive sleep I'd had in a while. I didn't want to be bothered with a wrong number. I tried to roll over and ignore it, but the phone kept ringing, piercing any hope I had of getting back to bed.

"What is it?!" I said into the receiver after I gave in and picked it up.

"He's gone down. Somewhere in China." It was Claire. The smoothness of her voice lulled me for a second until I comprehended the words.

"Put your TV on," she said.

I flicked on the tube just in time to hear the reporter in St. Louis say, "Hal, everyone here is very disappointed. They really thought he was gonna make it. At the same time, of course, they're thankful he is apparently unharmed."

"Thank you, Jeremy," the anchor said. " That was Jeremy Wingstadt reporting live from mission control in St. Louis. Now—this just in—we have some video taken several hours ago from the crash site. We're going to roll that for you now."

They rolled the footage and the TV went silent. I could hear Claire fidgeting on the other line.

"What does it look like," she said. "You have to tell me."

"Well, they're in China," I said. "I see Chinese. They're in a big field with rice paddies. It's soaking wet. There's water and a lot of mud everywhere. The balloon is stretched out across the field. It's silver and flapping in the wind. There are Chinese all around it. They're short, some of them wearing straw hats. They're smiling. They seem to be happy. The whole thing's a real scene for them, a real spectacle."

"Can you see him?" she said. "Is he there?"

"Yeah, there he is. He's standing in the rice paddies, gesturing, pointing to the balloon."

A new clip came up on the TV now. There was a microphone in front of the balloon guy. Finally, there was sound. "One of my propane burners blew out and I feared I wouldn't be able to keep her at an altitude high enough to make it over the mountains on the other side of this valley," he said. "Plus a fog was rolling in. I couldn't see. It was too risky. I looked for a soft, flat place to land and saw the rice field."

"What does he look like?" Claire said.

"He looks like an Air Force pilot, or maybe an astronaut," I said. "He's wearing a flight suit. His hair is all matted down and greasy. His head is kind of square-looking. He took his sunglasses off and keeps blinking. His eyes keep looking off to the side, as if he can't control them."

"It was the best thing to do," the defeated balloon man said. "I'm disappointed, but I'll be back. We'll try again. Better luck next time!"

The TV flicked back to the anchorman in the U.S. "And so ends one rich guy's quest for immortality in the sky," I thought I heard the newsman say. "We hope he'll try again soon to give us something to obsess over in the middle of the night. Otherwise we know your insomnia will become all the more frustrating."

Claire was quiet on the other end of the phone. Finally, she said, "So that's it, huh? I guess it was good while it lasted."

"I guess," I said.

"Well, good night," she said.

So that was it. The man flies 12,000 miles across the globe, lands on a rice paddy, smiles into the camera, and says, "Better luck next time!" This was an indignity. Failure was not supposed to be an option. We'd made it past Libya, sailed clear over India, fought a busted heater, feared we'd run out of fuel, suffered on military rations, sailed through and over storms in the middle of the ocean, and he lands in a "soft" rice field for safety's sake? It was too risky, he says?! Did he realize the world was counting on him? Couldn't he see the ramifications of his actions? You don't just bring her down because you're afraid. Suck it up, soldier! The multitudes are counting on you. How many sleepless nights did I waste on this guy?

I couldn't get his blinking eyes out of my head. He stood there in China, on the other side of the world, blinking into the camera, saying he couldn't see where he was going and he feared he'd crash into a mountain. Claire could have flown that balloon better than him and she can't see a damn thing! I wish he *had* crashed into a mountain. If you're not going to succeed, the only other way to be a hero is to die trying. You don't get second chances. At least, I never have.

I shut the TV off and headed out into the street. I'm not sure if it was gravity, or destiny, or stupidity that brought me there, but I ended up at Claire's apartment. I stood out in front of her door for a minute, wondering what I was doing. The place was completely dark. The curtains on the door were open, and the porch light gave me just enough light to see the dog sleeping in the shadows by the stairs. I rapped on the door and the dog started and barked. It jumped up and put its paws on the windowsill until Claire came down and shoved him aside.

"Who's there?" she said. "Steven, is that you? I told you, I'm not going."

"It's Charles," I said, a little surprised I called myself that. I fished for something to say, but nothing seemed appropriate. "I can't sleep again.

I knew you were still up."

She unlocked the door, held the dog back, and poked her head outside. "It's late," she said.

I pleaded. "I can't get this balloon guy out of my head. Please, can I just come in for a few minutes?"

She sighed and then pushed the door open. I followed her up the stairs. She didn't turn the light on this time. The TV was on, though, casting a bluish hue across the apartment. She sat down on the couch and faced the box. The Home Shopping Network was on. A woman was modeling rings. Her hand took up most of the TV screen.

I paced back and forth in the dim apartment for a few seconds, gathering my thoughts. Claire sat with her arms folded across her chest. Her hair was tied back. She wore boxer shorts and a long T-shirt. The dog relaxed and sat in the corner. Claire turned the volume down on the TV.

"Here's the thing," I said. "I want to explain why I ran out on you last week."

"You don't have to explain," she said. "I'm a blind woman. It's easy for people to run out on me. I can't very well run after them, can I?"

"That's got nothing to do with it," I said. "Really. You have to believe me."

I sat down beside her on the couch. They were hawking sunglasses on The Home Shopping Network now. A whole row of people stood there in dark, designer glasses. They all looked like they were blind to me.

"I've just been having a tough time," I said. "I'm not sleeping. I'm thinking about too many things. I feel stuck. I can't explain it, but I feel like there's cinder blocks tied to my feet, like I'm stuck in cement or something. I can't seem to do anything about it."

She turned toward me. Her glasses were off, but her eyes were closed, her head facing downward. She looked sad.

"There are some things going on in my mind," I said. "Maybe it is all in my head."

She put her hand on my shoulder and stroked my hair.

"I'm so damn tired," I said, and then I sank down into her lap, with my head resting on her thighs. She kept running her fingers gently through my hair.

"I thought he was going to make it," she said. "Your balloon man. He'd gone so far."

"I wish that had been me up there," I said. "I'm starting to think that I would have made it. That I never would have given up so easily if I had the chance he did."

Claire chuckled and kissed me on the head. "Imagine it," she said.

"It's a bright, sunny day and you're off with a puff and a whoosh, rising high above the ground, leaving everything else behind—except me. I'm there with you. We're leaving everything and everyone behind. We're rising up through the air. The wind is blowing against our faces and we can't stop giggling."

"Yeah, that's it," I said. I kissed her on the hand.

"Our balloon is called the Big Blue Morpho," she said. "It has a huge butterfly that spans almost its entire circumference. People laugh at us and say we're impractical, that this baby will never fly. But we don't care because we're proving them wrong, lifting off over a big cornfield, snubbing our noses at our doubters. We've got champagne and caviar, and we're toasting each other as we head higher."

I ran my lips over the length of her arm. "Keep going," I said.

"When we get high enough, I can see. I can see everything. I toss my stupid glasses and watch them fall to the ground. I can see the color of the sky, and I can see water in the distance. Best of all, I can see you. You're the best-looking man," she said and laughed. "You're quite the eye-candy in my fantasies," she said, giggling some more.

I kissed her neck now and I felt her quiver a little. "Don't stop," I said.

"It's so quiet at this altitude. We don't hear anything. Not even birds. Flying in our little box, our world is tranquil and we're content. Up here we don't gain weight, we don't need birth control, we don't get hung over. Up here, the Red Sox never lose to the Yankees. We don't ever have to sleep and we never get tired."

I took her shirt off and we lay down on the couch. She rolled over and I ran my hands up and down her back. "Keep going," I said.

"How high do you want to go?" she said.

"As far as you can take me."

"We cross over a great, blue ocean, and we rise higher and higher, above the clouds, heading closer and closer to space. We can see the stars above us. They look so close. Whole new galaxies look like they're within our reach. Going around the world isn't enough for us. We set out for the moon. It looks like a big, shining pearl from here."

I kissed the small of her back and slowly moved my lips toward her shoulders.

It's the smoothest, brightest thing I've ever seen," Claire said. "I can't wait to get there."

I ran my fingers through her hair, over her neck, and down her arms. I kissed her lower back again and inched up the length of her spine. Her skin was the smoothest I'd ever felt. I put my cheek against it and I could have just lain with my face pressed to her back for hours. I had to proceed to my final destination, though. I lifted my head. I took a deep breath and then came down with my lips square on the snarling sea horse. I kissed it long and hard and I could feel Claire writhing beneath me. I kissed it again and then I kissed all around it. I ran my hand over it. I traced it with my fingers. I nibbled at it, and then I kissed it some more. Finally, I nestled my face against the nape of her neck and I whispered in her ear, "It's beautiful. It's the most beautiful thing I've ever seen."

Then I shut my eyes. She rolled over, our lips finally met, and we were off and running right there on the couch. It was like I was running down a street with my eyes closed, Claire chasing behind me, saying, "Don't worry, you can do it. Just keep going, one foot after the other. Steady ahead now. You won't hit anything." In my fantasy, she was laughing and her dog was barking at me. I filled with nervous anticipation, afraid I would crash into a telephone pole, but I just kept going. I could hear my feet slapping against the pavement. I could feel the sweat pouring out of me and I could feel my muscles start to tighten, but it felt great. I breathed the cool air through my mouth and pulled it deep inside my body, holding it for as long as I could. I sucked everything in and kept it inside so I'd remember the moment. It was the fastest I'd moved in a long time. I didn't want to stop, so I just kept going, listening to the rhythm of my feet on the street, Claire watching me and cheering me on with each step I took.

"See, it's not so bad, is it?" she said.

"No," I said. "I think I can do this."

"I know you can," she said. "I've never had any doubt."

Pick Up Some Chinese,
My Only Son

Lorraine had never won anything in her life, so she was skeptical when the man from Louis' Thrift left a message on her answering machine saying she'd won a twenty-pound turkey in a Christmas drawing.

She was skeptical of the answering machine, too, which her son had given her two months ago for her sixty-first birthday. "A machine take my calls?" she had said, shortly after unwrapping the package. "What will my friends think if they have to talk to a machine?"

In front of her son, Roy, who was married now, with no children, she tried to create the impression that she had many friends who were always calling and keeping her busy with one thing or another. She did not want Roy, who lived in the suburbs now, an hour's drive through traffic, to worry that she was lonesome since her second husband had died, ten years now after Roy's father had died.

The truth was, however, that outside of Meredith Blackman, who lived upstairs and always smelled like bubble gum, there was no one left in Washington that Lorraine considered a friend. There were the people she new from Uhlman's Discount Furniture, where she worked as a cashier, but she really only considered them acquaintances, not friends. And then there was Gerald Polario, a salesman at Uhlman's who she considered neither a friend nor an acquaintance, but rather a threat to her womanly being. He'd asked her out every Friday night since her second husband died nearly a year ago. "I sold a recliner today, Lorraine," he would say. "Want to go to dinner tonight?" Or, "What do you think of that new love seat we got in, Lorraine? Do you have a *love* seat at your place?" he'd say, emphasizing the word *love*. She did not know how Gerald knew her husband had died, or how he knew she had been married for that matter. She never discussed her private life with her fellow employees and she didn't wear a wedding ring because she had arthritis and her fingers swelled up without warning. Gerald was not a good-looking man. He had crooked teeth and a thick mustache that always had crumbs of food stuck in it, and to top it off he talked too much. If none of these things were true, Lorraine might have considered going out with him because, as it was, the only social event she could count on regularly was when she went to the fire station with Meredith to play Beano on Saturday nights.

"This way you'll know I've called when you're not home," Roy had said about the answering machine. And with that remark, Lorraine became very proud of the bogus social life she'd created for Roy's benefit. She was always home when he called. Sometimes she would just let the phone ring so he would think she was out. It was all part of her effort to demonstrate that she didn't need him, not yet anyway. When she had broken her leg last year after falling from a chair which she stood upon to reach an old jar of gravy, Roy had asked her to quit her job and move in with him and Sherry, his wife. He made plenty of money to support the three of them. He worked for the Department of Defense, tracking missiles, or building them, or something to do with bombs—Lorraine wasn't quite sure what. But Roy and Sherry were practically newlyweds, and they didn't need Lorraine hanging around, infringing upon their privacy. And she didn't need them. She was perfectly fine living on her own.

Lorraine's mother had once told her that one's children become one's parents later in life. "It was a cycle," she said. "In a span of sixty years, you will go from child-bearing to child-rearing to being reared by your own children when your bones are too brittle to rear themselves." She had never had the chance to "rear" her mother, since her mother died in her thirties, but Lorraine was damn sure Roy would not be her provider and care-giver anytime soon. Besides, Roy lived in Virginia, like the rest of the people who worked for DOD (as Roy called it whenever he spoke about where he worked), and what would she do in Virginia?

So, for nearly two months, the answering machine sat, still packed in its box, right there on the countertop next to the phone, until, finally, she set aside an entire Saturday afternoon to open it and learn how to work it.

The directions were tedious, printed so small she had to squint with her glasses on, and they called for her to speak into this machine to leave her own message in anticipation of those who would call and want to speak to the machine instead of her. She tried to be creative and think up her own outgoing message, but faltered each time she pressed the record button: "Ahh . . . Ahh . . . This is Lorraine . . . Ahh . . . Ahh . . . This is my new machine. . . . Ahh . . . Ahh." She replayed her recording and decided she sounded like Mr. Montaigne, the widower next door, who in recent months had taken to moaning and wailing at night. "Ahh!" she would hear through the wall. "Ahh! Ahh!" And then, "Ohhhh. Oh." She didn't know what was wrong with him. At first she thought he might even be engaging in some kind of sexual activity. But as it continued she realized he was moaning from some kind of pain that seemed to affect him more at night.

So she gave up trying to come up with something of her own and she resorted to reading the prepared statement included with the instruction manual, which, surprisingly, she did in one try without stuttering or stammering: "Hello. This is Lorraine. I am unable to take your phone call right now. Please leave your name, telephone number, time you called, and a brief message after the tone."

When she played it back, she winced at the sound of her voice. The only other time she remembered being recorded was when Roy did a project for school in which he interviewed her about her life and asked for her opinions on Nazis and communists and Koreans and the Vietnamese. Everything the boy was interested in had to do with war or preparing for war. She remembered answering his questions slowly, methodically, thinking about her answers before she spoke them. And she remembered that her voice sounded much smoother and much more lady-like than it did now. Now she almost sounded like a man. Her voice was rough and husky, as if she smoked cigarettes, but she didn't, or, at least, hadn't in twenty years. She sounded older than she was and wondered what she could do to make her voice sound more gentle.

Once the counter was dusted and the answering machine all set up, she stared at its tiny red light, which was flat and still now but supposed to flash intermittently when there was a message. For a time, she even pulled her chair next to the counter and sat there a while waiting for the phone to ring. Her plan was to let the machine pick up the next time someone— most likely Roy—called and then call him back later in the day and say she had been downtown at a restaurant with friends. But nobody called for four days, not even Meredith because she usually came by unannounced anyway.

On Tuesday she had a strong feeling, a premonition, she thought, that someone had left her a message while she was at work. She raced home with visions of the flashing red light in her head, nearly tripped going into her apartment, and dropped her coat on the floor as she tramped into the kitchen to examine the machine. The light was unmoving, same as it was the day before. She paced back and forth for a minute, her heels clicking across the linoleum. She was desperate to hear something, anything, so she replayed her own outgoing message, but halfway before it finished she turned the volume down. She couldn't stand the sound of her raspy voice.

A little later, Meredith came by, rapping on her door, asking if she could come in for tea, but Lorraine snapped at her and told her not to come down again without calling her over the phone first. "How am I supposed to know if the machine works?" Lorraine muttered to herself. "Damn bubble gum woman too lazy to pick up the phone and call before she comes bothering me."

So, on Wednesday, when it finally happened, when her machine finally picked up a call, she was no longer prepared for it. She had even made it a point to avoid the answering machine when she came home. It wasn't until halfway through her dinner that she noticed the blinking light. She jumped up and stood beside the countertop. "What are you all excited about, Lorraine?" she said out loud. "It's probably just Meredith."

She pressed the play button, hoping to hear Roy. But the man's voice that spoke to her was one she had never heard before. He spoke slowly and quietly, as if he didn't want anyone else to hear him, and he droned on like the hum of Lorraine's old refrigerator, leaving an extra long message. She had to rewind it once to take it all in, but the essence of the recording was this: she had won first prize in a Christmas raffle, a twenty-pound Butterball turkey. She remembered buying the ticket for a dollar from Gretta, the other cashier at work. First prize was the turkey, second prize was a ten-pound spiral ham, and third prize, was a basket of jam. Lorraine didn't expect to win anything, but she bought a ticket anyway because the raffle was a fundraiser for homeless people, and Lord knew there were enough of them, all deserving of some kind of Christmas meal. Besides, Gretta was a good woman, a little overweight, but more generous than most; she spent three evenings a week serving food at a shelter off of Georgia Avenue. One raffle ticket was the least Lorraine could do.

But it was mid-January now and she had completely forgotten about the drawing. For a minute she thought the phone call might be a prank. Someone from work must have seen her buying the ticket and was trying to put one over on her. But the man on the machine, named Lester Hodgkins, clearly identified himself as an employee of Louis' Thrift, giving detailed directions as to where she should go to pick up the turkey. But it was the last thing Mr. Hodgkins said, or rather, the way he said it that convinced Lorraine he was genuine. "I thank you, Mrs. Hovington," he said, speaking a little louder, with a slight intonation in his voice, "for your support. Your charitable act and the gifts of others helped make this a brighter holiday season for many less-fortunates."

She had helped many "less-fortunates." She'd never thought of calling them that. She called them poor or homeless or street people or drunks. "Less-fortunates" sounded so much nicer. There were "less-fortunates" out there who didn't have a son in Virginia, or their own apartment in the city, or a job at a furniture store. After those last words, the machine beeped and clicked until Lorraine began to fear something was wrong with it. All of a sudden it went quiet, as if it were dead, but then the steady red light reappeared again. Lorraine sat down in her chair by the window to ponder her newly found fortune. She was giddy with excitement and decided next week she would buy a lottery ticket to try her hand at winning money—which she expected would be a much more difficult task, even if she was on a lucky streak. She didn't want to go overboard, but she would at least buy three game cards instead of her regular two at Beano this weekend.

Her prize, however, would cause some complications in her life and she had to find a way to minimize them. First off, Mr. Hodgkins had instructed her to pick up the turkey, which was in deep-freeze at Louis' Thrift, between the hours of nine and five, Monday through Friday. This posed a problem because of work. She would have to take an extended lunch hour and she could never tell how the moody Mr. Robillard, the acting manager, would react. But she had more tenure at Uhlman's than him and she would go over his head if he gave her any flak.

The second problem was that Louis' Thrift was located way out off of Minnesota Avenue in a part of town that she was uncertain of. She hadn't been there in years, since before they built the subway even. But she watched the Channel 5 news every night. People were dying of unnatural causes every day in this city. Helena Simms, the anchorwoman, reported about shootings every day, and she always did it with that annoying smirk on her face and the perkiness of some of the morning anchorwomen, as if she were relaying how one crocheted or how one could make a low-fat chocolate mousse for dessert. "Just ahead in today's news," she would say, "a gunman opens fire on a public swimming pool, killing two children and wounding three others. The Orioles take on the Yankees at Camden Yards, and will Bob promise us more sunshine tomorrow? Stay tuned."

She wasn't sure how bad the neighborhood would be where Louis' Thrift was located, but she was determined not to let fear keep her from the turkey. She considered asking someone to go with her. Gerald Polario would certainly love the opportunity to accompany her anywhere, but how would that look if the two of them went off together during their lunch hour? And then he'd probably think he'd earned the right to come over for turkey dinner; this she could not allow.

Roy would probably be willing to go with her if she asked, but she would never ask him. Then there was always Meredith, but Lorraine couldn't imagine she would be much of a deterrent from trouble. And she wouldn't be much help carrying the turkey, either.

She deliberated about how to get this Butterball for over a week and at one point almost abandoned the whole idea. But visions of turkey breast, and turkey salad sandwiches, and turkey soup filled her head until, finally, she decided, for better or worse, to go alone to Southeast Washington and find Louis' Thrift on her own.

She made all the preparations the night before her excursion. She pulled her grocery cart out of the closet and oiled the wheels. She picked out the clothes she'd wear, including her most comfortable pair of walking shoes, slacks with an elastic waistband, and her pomegranate hat with the pigeon feather in it. Lastly, she boiled a concoction of black tea, honey, and lemon before she went to sleep, and she sipped it in bed while watching the ten o'clock news. She drank this in hope that it would soothe her throat and her voice would not sound so rough the next day. She wouldn't mind having a voice like Helena Simms on the TV, as long as a voice like that didn't automatically make one smile while saying, "A fourteen-year-old girl was stabbed today at a convenience store on Seventh Street, Southeast."

Lorraine fell asleep thinking about the turkey, but she was woken at quarter to eleven by Mr. Montaigne, moaning in pain next door. This was a trend that had become increasingly alarming to Lorraine. Mr. Montaigne was an ailing man no doubt, but ailing of what she had no idea, and that was the worst part of it for her: listening to this man wail in the dark, never knowing why he did it. Recently, she had begun to imagine he had tumors on his back and on his arms, and whenever he moved they caused him great agony. The situation might have grown so bad that he couldn't even lay down peacefully anymore, and that was why his affliction became so noticeable at night, his loud, painful wail waking her up at random hours. Then she wouldn't be able to fall back to sleep, and she would sit up in bed having to listen to the grunts and the cries, sometimes quick and high-pitched, sometimes longer and deep-sounding, rising from deep within his chest. Sometimes he sounded like his spleen or some other internal organ was being ripped from his body. The sounds frightened her, and she would put the TV on very loud to drown them out and lie there with a pillow over her face. She did this now, but the only thing on was the eleven o'clock news and she was forced to listen to another anchorwoman report how, earlier in the evening, an old woman had been bludgeoned to death for four dollars and a charm bracelet.

She turned the TV off and chose to listen to the moans coming from next door. They would subside and she would nearly fall back to sleep again, and then there would be a sharp yelp or two, like a dog that had just been hit by a car. She imagined Mr. Montaigne lying in bed, trying to get up, but each time he moved being overcome by excruciating agony. There were times when she even thought about calling the apartment manager, or the police, or an ambulance. But now she just sat up in bed and said sternly, "Mr. Montaigne? Mr. Montaigne!" She had no idea if he could hear her through the walls, but the noise subsided and she was left in silence thinking about him. He was only in his early seventies; she couldn't imagine that in ten years she herself would be wailing like him in the middle of the night. She would rather be bludgeoned to death for four dollars and a charm bracelet, and she fell asleep thinking about that.

In the morning, the struggle with Mr. Montaigne the night before seemed rather distant as she anticipated her trip to get the turkey. She got ready to go quickly, but before she left for work she felt the need to do one more thing: change the message on her answering machine. She wasn't sure why today, of all days, she had to do this, but she stood solemnly above the machine, staring at the red light as if she were about to recite her last will and testament. She pressed the button and then spoke as coherently as she could: "This is Lorraine. I am out right now. I plan to return today. But one never knows if one will be bludgeoned in the head, and should that happen to me today, I may not be able to return your call."

Lorraine fidgeted about her cash register all morning at Uhlman's, continually reviewing her plan of transport to Louis' Thrift. Mr. Hodgkins had recommended she take the subway and then transfer to a bus that would bring her to within walking distance of the thrift store. But, Lorraine had combed through all her bus schedules and found she could get to the same location by taking only buses, and transferring only twice. She was relieved not to have to take the subway. The subway made her dizzy. It traveled too fast, and she didn't like being trapped in a tunnel. As she sped by those dim lights that gently illuminated the concrete walls, she could not help but feel the subway was an abnormal mode of transportation. She felt like she were traveling in a spaceship, and she firmly believed that man was not made to travel in space.

When she was satisfied that she had memorized her bus transfer points, she began checking her watch every five minutes, counting down to twelve noon when she would grab her coat, hat, and grocery cart, and be out the door before anyone could ask her any questions. Of course, she wasn't quick enough for Gerald Polario, who stood in front of the door as she tried to leave and said, "What's the grocery cart for, Lorraine?"

"Now is that the kind of question to ask a lady?" was all Lorraine said, and she pushed past him and got herself out into the street.

Her first bus was four minutes late, which made her uptight about how long this whole errand was going to take, but after she found a seat she took a couple deep breaths and tried to relax. She even took her watch off and put it inside her coat pocket. This was a trip for her, an excursion to a part of the city she hadn't visited in a long time. She would do her best to forget her nervous apprehension and take it all in, enjoy it. After all, this was why she lived in the city and not in Virginia with Roy.

*   *   *

She could smell exhaust fumes on the second bus she rode, and that, combined with the regular bumps and bounces of the road, made her sleepy. She let herself close her eyes, and she dozed but woke up with a start, fearing she might miss her stop. She opened her eyes wide, yawned and bit her lower lip, trying to keep herself awake. The child in the seat in front of her was up on his knees, facing her, his mouth pressed against the support bar that Lorraine had used to steady herself while she sat down. An extraordinarily copious amount of saliva covered the boy's lips and the railing. She smiled at him, thinking of all the germs he was ingesting. She wanted to wipe his mouth and say something to him, but she was afraid her voice would scare him. The tea and honey mixture had done nothing to soothe its coarseness and she decided now that she regretted getting the answering machine. If Roy had never given it to her, she never would have heard what she sounded like.

The child's mother hoisted him up on her lap, leaving Lorraine staring at a spittle of drool hanging from the safety bar. She had half a mind to wipe it up with her handkerchief, but it wasn't her responsibility. Why should she clean up after someone else's child? Lord knows, she'd cleaned up after her own child long enough. That part of her life was done now; she was free of it. With her son's marriage, she had finally regained the independence she had once possessed some forty years ago. She had to keep reminding herself that she had planned it this way. Mitchell, Roy's father, had wanted two more children. It was his hope that she would bear three children in five years. But she had told him she needed recovery time. He would have to wait. Then, when five years passed and she still was not ready to have another child, he pleaded with her. She said no, sure that another child would be the end of her, and their marriage was never quite the same. On his deathbed, she wept and one of the last things she said to him was an apology for not bearing him another child. Would one more have killed her? She could have endured it for his sake. Or did she just not love Mitchell enough to have another child with him? It was a question that still plagued her and she had probably married again in an attempt to escape her guilt. She clearly had not been ready for marriage a second time. At least by then she was too old to be thinking about another child, though sometimes those kinds of thoughts crept up on her: did she miss out on her own womanhood by not having more children?

But she tried not to allow herself to feel guilty over the path she'd chosen, and she would not feel guilty for her husbands' death like some widows. They were six feet under and, as much as she loved them or didn't love them, all she could do was keep their memory alive and go on with her life—which she was determined to do. Just getting on this bus and going to Minnesota Avenue proved she was moving on, doing what she wanted. Provided she wasn't being "parented" by Roy, she could get on a bus and go anywhere she wanted. Today, Minnesota Avenue, tomorrow, the White House, the next day, the National Gallery. Then, when the weather got warmer she'd be off to Virginia Beach or Ocean City, where she would sit along the boardwalk like she did as a teenager, and she'd smile at men she didn't know—good-looking men, not Gerald Polario—then turn away bashfully if they smiled back.

She tried to imagine what Mr. Hodgkins of Louis' Thrift might look like. His voice was quiet and deliberate, but those were not necessarily bad qualities in a man. She imagined him being tall and thin, with dark hair cut very short. Of course, any time she fantasized about a man, he was tall and thin, with dark hair cut very short. Anthony Perkins was a man she was dreadfully attracted to. Even after she saw him in a movie where he dressed up like one woman and stabbed another in a shower, she still thought he was a very attractive man.

She hoped Mr. Hodgkins would be attractive, but she kept thinking about his name. She was pretty sure there was something called Hodgkin's disease, and she didn't know how serious a condition it was but she envisioned someone who had it would be sickly with tumors and thinning hair. And by association she feared that Mr. Hodgkins might be ill, and she was not interested or capable of caring for anyone right now. If he was ill, she would not be susceptible to any charm he might possess by being tall and thin with short dark hair.

She did not ride on the third bus for very long before her stop came up. Her grocery cart clanged down the steps of the bus and, despite her more relaxed mood, she stepped into the street with some trepidation. The day was overcast and the low clouds cast gray shadows over the buildings in front of her, making them seem more drab than they might have been. There were not many people out, and she had plenty of room to maneuver her grocery cart between the pigeon droppings and black wads of gum that had not been scraped from the sidewalk. A few "less-fortunates" milled about—perhaps people she had helped to feed on Christmas by buying her raffle ticket—and every so often someone would walk past her and her grip would tighten on the cart as she sized him up, trying to determine if he was the type who would shoot an old woman in the head or bludgeon her to death for four dollars and a charm bracelet.

There were a couple of undeveloped lots that had been allowed to degenerate over time. Small piles of rubble—pipes, bricks, broken glass—lay on sandy, barren property, which reminded Lorraine of the scenery in old cowboy movies she had watched. She would not have been surprised to see Doc Holiday strolling about with a pistol slung around his hip.

But this was far from a ghost town. There were many of the same businesses that inhabited her own neighborhood: Seven-Eleven, CVS, Safeway. There were liquor stores and dry cleaners, a couple of run-down bars with no windows, a video shop with dirty movies.

And there were martial arts schools—more martial arts schools than she'd ever seen in one place. There was Tyrone's Tai Chi, Flying Dragon's Aikido, and Gentle Yim's Kung Fu all within a three-block radius. She had no idea what the difference was between, say karate and taekwondo, and she wondered if a kung fu master killed someone differently than an expert in tai chi. Her only experience with the martial arts came after Roy begged her to let him take karate lessons when he was twelve. After much contemplation, she allowed it, and on a few Saturday mornings took the bus with him to a little studio near Nineteenth and N where she watched him throw kicks and shout strange sounds for an hour and a half. The whole thing scared her as she watched her son become like an animal, hissing, wheezing, and clenching his teeth in front of the mirror at home, and she was glad to have an excuse to pull him out of the class when, on the third week, another boy, a vicious, little runt of a boy, swung around and kicked Roy in the mouth. Lorraine had run right onto their practice mat, shoved the other boy to the floor, grabbed Roy by the hand and dragged him out of there. Of course, he protested and when he struggled to break her grasp, her favorite white blouse was stained with blood. But his gums bled all day, and he ended up lying there in bed for hours with cotton shoved in his mouth. And every thirty minutes or so Lorraine would stand in the doorway to his room and say, "You're not going back there. Never! Do you hear me?"

But now, privately, she thought if people were going to try to kill each other, karate would be a much more dignified way of going about it. She imagined Helena Simms on the Channel 5 news smiling into the camera saying, "A twenty-eight-year-old man was killed today after a swift kick to the temple. There was no mess, and no one killed in the crossfire." Lorraine imagined if karate were the number-one cause of killing rather than guns, the murder rate in the District would drop from over four hundred a year to somewhere in the low one hundreds.

She was certainly in a high-crime area, and she wondered if all these self-defense places really were a product of market forces. She didn't see how any blackbelt could stand much chance against a semi-automatic weapon, but if the people who participated in these classes achieved the illusion that they could protect themselves, then most likely they also achieved a sense of control over their lives. And if that were the case, she wondered if she weren't too old yet to learn aikido and considered stopping in on one of the studios. But after walking another block, she thought better of it. She knew she'd never be able to subscribe fully to the illusion.

Evidently, Louis' Thrift was not an entity unto itself. Louis apparently owned the whole block. There was a Louis' Discount Rugs on the corner, and Louis' Thrift was in between Louis' Drugs and, yes, Louis' Martial Arts Instruction. The thrift store was the smallest shop in the plaza, with a hand-painted sign taped to its window that said "QUALITY THRIFT MERCHANDISE AND APPAREL FOR OVER TEN YEARS." The display next to the sign included an electric blender, a tattered copy of *Moby Dick*, and a man's polyester suit with a fake carnation in its breast pocket, hanging from a wire hanger attached to a suction-cup hook that was stuck to the window.

Lorraine walked into the store and her grocery cart got caught in the door as it slammed shut behind her. A little bell kept jingling as she freed the cart, and all the while the man who sat at the counter never even flinched. Lorraine thought he looked just a few years younger than her. He sat upon a high stool, with his elbows propped up on the countertop and his chin resting in his hands. He was reading a book, or at least, from Lorraine's vantage point, staring at it thoughtfully as if he were trying to comprehend something. He didn't even look up at her, and for a second she thought he might even be deaf.

She pushed her cart in front of her and walked down one of the aisles, surveying the store, pretending she was shopping. There were racks of clothes, which seemed to be assembled in no particular order—not even men's separated from women's. There was a bin filled completely with toasters—large ones, small ones, toasters with two slots, toasters with four slots, toaster ovens. If she ever needed a new toaster, she would come back here—although the thought of using a toaster that still might have some stranger's toast crumbs stuck in it repulsed her. These days, when you bought second-hand products, you didn't know what diseases you were buying with them. There were stacks of black ashtrays like the ones people used at the fire station during Beano on Saturday nights. There were plates with pictures of dogs and cats and former President Reagan on them. There were boxes of clip-on earrings and racks of shoes that smelled like other people's feet. There were plastic pink flamingos. And there was a table of children's toys, with mangled stuffed animals and G.I. Joe dolls missing limbs and clothes.

Roy had had a large collection of G.I. Joes that he used to stage war games with in which he crunched them under Tonka trucks and ripped their heads off and then hog-tied the surviving dolls and imprisoned them in a stockade made of Popsicle sticks and pipe cleaners. One day Lorraine caught him lighting matches under the survivors' feet until their shoes began to melt and she set out on a campaign to wean her son from yet another violent activity by telling him that playing with G.I. Joes was no better than playing with Barbie dolls. And what would his friends say if they knew he played with Barbie dolls? So, shortly afterward, he abandoned the G.I. Joes and began combing Rock Creek Park with a B.B. gun, hunting for birds and squirrels and whatever other small animals he could find and maim. That was when she started talking to the school psychologist who insisted that nothing Roy did was abnormal for a boy his age. But she insisted that the psychologist evaluate her son, and when the psychologist's evaluation claimed Roy had no mental problems, Lorraine took matters into her own hands. She painted his room a lavender blue because she'd read that certain colors could change a person's personality, and she fed him prunes, and she took him to see movies that were about well-adjusted teenagers or animals that brought out the good in everyone. And by the time he graduated from high school, Lorraine noticed that her son was, indeed, normal, and she deserved credit for his upbringing and she deserved a rest. Only she rested right through his college years, and then when he went on for his master's and then his Ph.D. she was never even really sure what he was studying. To her, all that mattered was that one day he be able to put a *Dr.* in front of his name. And then right under her nose he started working for the Pentagon and she knew all that aggression surely had been stored up inside of him and she must not have been as good a mother as she thought.

She looked up at the man behind the counter, who still sat in the same position, staring at the book, and a feeling came over her that she could not understand. Her heart started racing and she felt her face becoming flushed. She checked one more time to make sure the man wasn't looking, then she grabbed a G.I. Joe, snapped one of its legs off, and shoved it, foot and all, into her coat pocket. She had no idea why she did this, but the action exhilarated her. She felt like a schoolgirl and she became giddy; she kept her face turned away from the man at the counter for fear he would see her smirking. "I have to get my damn turkey and get out of here," she thought to herself, laughing to herself.

"Excuse me," she said, still half-wondering if the man behind the counter might be deaf. There was no one else in the store, and no sound except for occasional yells and grunts coming from the martial arts school next door. For a second, she felt queasy like she had the night before as the sounds emanating from Louis' Martial Arts Instruction sounded like some of the wails of Mr. Montaigne—quick jabs that trailed off into silence. But as she listened more closely she could make out the familiar warring cry Roy used to use during his karate stage. "Kee-ya," it sounded like to her. "Kee-ya!" *Kee-ya* for a blow to the head. *Kee-ya* for a roundhouse kick. *Kee-ya* for an elbow to the chest. Helena Simms on the ten o'clock news: "And with a loud *kee-ya* the assailant broke the victim's neck. Only the ninety-first homicide in the District this year. Way below our average."

The man at the counter finally looked up at her. To her surprise, he even had a slight welcoming smile on his face.

"I'm Lorraine Hovington," Lorraine said, squeezing the G.I. Joe leg in her pocket. "I came to pick up a turkey I won in a Christmas drawing."

"Mrs. Hovington, Mrs. Hovington," he said, "a pleasure to meet you." He climbed off his stool, came out in front of the counter and shook her hand. "I hope you found us all right. I'm Lester Hodgkins."

So, this was Mr. Hodgkins, Lorraine thought. He was no Anthony Perkins. He was thin, but he was shorter than her, and he had thinning, greasy, brown hair that he would push back into place when it fell onto his forehead. He wore a green vest that was too large for him and tan trousers that hung too loosely off his hips. But he did not display any outstanding signs of illness or tumors.

"How do you do, Mr. Hodgkins. Thank you for your directions. I really had no trouble at all."

"I'm glad to hear it. We are kind of tucked out of the way here."

Yes, she wanted to say, hidden amongst the kung fu establishments. She wondered if vandals and thieves were less apt to disturb kickboxers and their neighbors.

Mr. Hodgkins went back behind the counter and sorted through a stack of papers. "I just have to have you sign a slip for receipt of the turkey. You're the first to come. The ham and the jam have not been picked up yet."

His voice was smooth and quiet like it was on the answering machine, though less monotone in person. He gave her a piece of paper to sign and then went into the back room. Lorraine readied her grocery cart. She was at the midway point of her journey. Soon she'd be back at work and Louis' Thrift would be just a memory. But Mr. Hodgkins took longer than she expected. He was making all kinds of noise in the back. Doors were being opened and closed; things were being moved around. There was clanging and banging and then the sound of something being dragged across the floor. He'd better not be dragging my turkey, Lorraine thought to herself.

While she waited, she moved in closer to the counter and tried to get a look at the book Mr. Hodgkins had been reading. It lay flat on the counter, opened to the first page of a chapter right in the middle of the book. She peered in closer and read the chapter title: "The Setting and Ministry of Jesus." This Mr. Hodgkins didn't seem to be the holy roller type, but one could never tell. Lorraine herself was ambivalent about religion. She had gone to church every Sunday as a child, but by the time she got married she'd given up on it. The only time she wished she'd stuck with it was when she had to teach Roy right from wrong. She never had the opportunity to simply say to him, "God does not want you destroying his beloved creatures when you're marauding through the park."

That would make a fine headline on the evening news. Helena Simms: "A crack dealer in Anacostia surrendered a semi-automatic weapon to police officers today, citing God's commandment *Thou shalt not kill* as reason enough not to go on murdering."

Lorraine leaned in closer to the book again and tried to read the first line of the first paragraph, but then she heard Mr. Hodgkins coming back. He rolled the turkey in on a squeaky dolly and just as he got in front of her one of its wheels caught on the edge of the counter. The dolly stopped and the turkey flew forward, bouncing in front of Lorraine's feet like a cinder block.

"Whoa, that's one solid bird you got there, Mrs. Hovington," Mr. Hodgkins said. "Frozen right through."

He bent over and hoisted the turkey up onto Lorraine's cart and then he stood there hunched over, out of breath. He was bowlegged and it struck Lorraine that he looked like an ape as he remained there hovering over the turkey.

"Thank you, Mr. Hodgkins," she said as she strapped the turkey into the cart. But he said nothing; his teeth were clinched and she could hear the air whistling in and out of his nose as he looked down at her. Finally, he flipped his bangs off his forehead again.

Lorraine could feel the cold coming off the turkey and she knocked her fist against it. It would take a full day to thaw. But it was a fine bird, beautifully plump and round. She already envisioned it sitting in her oven, roasting until it was a perfect brown, juicy and savory. She hadn't cooked a whole turkey in years and now, as she thought about it, she longed to do it.

She stood up and rested her hands atop the cart. "So, did the raffle raise much money?" she asked, but Mr. Hodgkins appeared not to hear her. He was staring lecherously at the turkey.

"Pardon? I'm sorry," he finally said.

"The raffle. How did it go?"

"Wonderful, wonderful. Our best ever. We were able to buy forty-five meals with the money."

"That is wonderful. I'm glad."

"Yes," he said and looked at her oddly, his head twitching a bit.

Lorraine could think of nothing else to say, so she thanked him again and then headed for the door. But he called to her and then came over to her. She thought he was going to open the door for her, but instead he held out his hand. And when she shook it he took his other hand as well and clasped it around hers.

"Thank you very, very much, Lorraine," he said, making eye contact with her that made her very uncomfortable. She tasted his stale breath in her mouth and she turned away as quickly as she could.

"I hope we see you again, sometime," he said.

"Certainly," she said, looking around the room, checking to make sure there hadn't, indeed, been someone else there the whole time.

She had hoped he would at least help her out of the store, but his hair had fallen to his forehead again and he shoved it back into place one more time, then stood there smiling while she struggled with the door. Lorraine was relieved once she got outside. She could not say she thought very highly of Mr. Hodgkins. But she felt sorry for him. She thought he might be the type of person who lay awake moaning in bed in the middle of the night.

"Goodbye," she heard him say. She looked up at the polyester suit in the window one more time and then took off for the bus stop, towing the turkey behind her.

Getting the turkey home safely worried her more than finding Louis' Thrift. Now she had something to lose. What could she possibly do to anyone who set upon her turkey and tried to take it away from her? Before getting on the first bus, she made sure the straps that held down the turkey were secure. At the very least, no one would be able to swipe it out of the cart. They'd have to take the whole cart and her along with it.

She got on each of her buses backwards, lifting the turkey ever so gently up the steps, one at a time. A gentleman tried to help her once and she politely declined. "I've got it," she said. "Thank you anyway." She didn't want to take the risk of any strangers touching it. On the first bus she took the turkey out of the cart and heaved it into the seat next to her. Several people kept looking at her and the turkey, and at one point she even draped her coat over the bird to protect it from strangers' stares. She was just glad it wasn't rush hour; the bus wasn't crowded and there was nobody to ask the turkey to give up its seat. On the next bus, she thought better of it, though, and she held the turkey in her lap. After a while its coldness began to sting her hands and its weight made her legs ache, but she endured it. One had to endure life's hardships if one was going to get any joy out of it. With sixty-one years behind her and the turkey in her lap, she was beginning to become more certain of that.

When the third bus dropped her off near Uhlman's, she reached into her pocket to get her watch and accidentally pulled out G.I. Joe's leg. She had forgotten all about it and now laughed out loud as she squeezed it in her hand. When she finally put her watch back on it was nearly two o'clock. The whole ordeal had taken just under two hours. She walked into Uhlman's pushing the turkey ahead of her, checking it every so often to make sure it was okay.

She spread her coat out on a recliner facing her cash register and placed the turkey on it. This way she could see it at all times as it underwent the thawing process. She had things to worry about, too. Gerald Polario definitely had eyes for the turkey. He circled it like a hawk and finally squatted down and studied it closely.

"That's a mighty fine bird you've got there, Lorraine," he said.

"Don't touch it," Lorraine said, ready to leap around the counter if he got any closer.

"Well, are you gonna need any help dressing this turkey? I'd certainly be willing to offer my services."

This suggestion infuriated Lorraine more than anything else Gerald had ever said to her. The thought of sharing this prized possession with him was enough to turn her stomach, and she almost told him so, but didn't want to create a ruckus. She didn't want to risk irking Mr. Robillard further, for fear that he might make her take the turkey to the storage room.

"Just back away from it, Gerald," she said, taking a step closer to him to show she meant business.

Gerald got up and went back to work, but thereafter every time he walked by Lorraine silently hissed at him and gave him the evil eye. She guarded the turkey for the rest of the day, watching the condensation build up as it thawed. Then the minute her shift was up, the turkey was back in her carriage and she made the trip home without incident.

At home, she put the turkey in a pan on the counter, but propped it up so it wouldn't be laying on its back; and, as she made her dinner of leftover split-pea soup and American chop suey, no matter where she stood in the kitchen the turkey seemed to face her. Every so often as she walked by she tapped it lovingly on its frozen midsection. During one of these passes she noticed the light on her answering machine was blinking and a rush of joy swept through her. Call number two! she thought. Perhaps she should begin to log her calls so she would have records of who called her and when. From now on, she might even let the machine answer the phone while she was home. There was something dignified about not answering someone's call, but returning it later.

She pressed the message button and the machine clicked and beeped until finally a recording was being played but no one was talking. There was someone breathing—a whistling kind of breathing—but whoever it was didn't say anything. This went on for several seconds until she heard it, she distinctively heard it: the sound of *kee-ya* reverberating in the background. Then there was a loud clunk and the line was disconnected.

A chill ran through Lorraine. It was the Hodgkins man from Louis' Thrift—she was sure of it. He had her phone number. He had called last week. What did he want? Did he know she had stolen one of his G.I. Joe's legs? She went to her coat and found the leg. It was a stupid thing to do, she thought. She didn't know what came over her. But he couldn't have seen her take it. He couldn't have. She tossed the leg in the kitchen drawer with her flashlight and candles, wondering what else Mr. Hodgkins could have wanted. He was a strange man who looked at her very strangely before she'd left the store. And he had his eyes on her turkey the same way Gerald Polario had. It was possible that he was calling to ask if he, too, could join her for dinner. Why did unsavory men want a piece of her turkey? She was sure that if Mr. Hodgkins had the gall of Gerald Polario he would have tried to invite himself over for dinner. But as it was, Mr. Hodgkins was even more socially inept than Gerald and he just sat there breathing on the phone. Either that or he was really a pervert. For a second she was frightened, but then she thought better of it. She could handle Mr. Hodgkins. She just hoped he didn't call again.

However, as she began to think about how to prepare the turkey, she also wondered whether or not she should share it with anyone. For sure, she would make her turkey pot pie and her turkey salad, but she thought she should first have a real turkey dinner with all the trimmings. Tomorrow she would go shopping and buy candied yams, cranberry sauce, potatoes, celery for stuffing, and anything else she might want at the time. She could invite Roy over, but it would sound pathetic of her to ask her son and his wife to come all the way from Virginia to share a turkey with her when it was seven months from Thanksgiving. She'd do better to tell Roy she had friends over for one huge, delicious feast. And she could also give him a detailed account of her journey to get the turkey. That was no small accomplishment, and it would further solidify her independence and competence in his mind.

There was always Meredith. She would certainly enjoy such a meal, and she would appreciate it, too. That was one thing about Meredith—she always expressed her thankfulness when you did something for her, even if she almost took it to the point of being annoying. So, that was what she'd do—go shopping in the morning (it would be Saturday, after all), cook all day, and invite Meredith over for dinner.

She ate her chop suey and recounted the day's experience, then she washed up and watched television until she fell asleep. Mr. Montaigne only woke her up once during the night. It was about 2:00 a.m. and the sounds he was making were like a violent, exaggerated sneeze. Lorraine clasped her hands over her ears. Soon she fell back to sleep, but at some point during the night she dreamed of Mr. Montaigne. The two of them were sitting outside on the porch of a big house. Mr. Montaigne swayed back and forth in a rocking chair. He had a large tumor bulging out of his neck. Somehow, Lorraine was not repulsed by this. She quietly held a doll in her lap, brushing its long, blonde hair. In the front yard, not more than twenty feet from the porch, children kicked a ball lazily back and forth. In her dream, Lorraine knew these children, but in her memory, she had no idea who they were, and the whole time she and Mr. Montaigne never said a word to each other.

*   *   *

In the morning, before she left for Safeway, she went upstairs to invite Meredith to dinner, but she was not home and her door was locked. So, Lorraine did her shopping and, when she returned, toting her bag of groceries, she found the answering machine flashing. She hoped it was Meredith; she didn't want to be looking for her all day. She put the groceries in the refrigerator first, purposely prolonging her anticipation, then adjusted the volume and pressed the playback button. Perhaps it was Roy, she thought. It was not unlike him to call on a Saturday morning. But what she heard sounded exactly like the last message she'd received: whistling breathing and a faint *kee-ya* in the background. Lorraine took a step back from the machine, stunned that someone would do this to her. Mr. Hodgkins really must be a freak, she thought. Only he disguises it by posing with religious books and volunteering for charity. She had half a mind to call Louis' Thrift right now and let him have it. But she knew there was only one thing she could do to prevent this sort of thing from happening again.

She grabbed the answering machine off the counter, yanked its cord out of the wall, and stashed the whole thing in her cupboard with her CB scanner, Salad Shooter, air popcorn popper, and the rest of the electrical appliances she never used.

"What a wretched man," she said out loud. But then she calmed herself down. There was no need to go on about it. She had gotten what she wanted from him—her lovely turkey—and she never had to see him again.

She took the turkey out of the refrigerator and struggled to lift it to the countertop, but she did it without spilling any of the juice that had leaked out of the bird. She squeezed it in several different spots to make sure it was completely thawed. It was soft all over and she massaged its skin, preparing it for the oven. She took out its innards and carefully wrapped them in a plastic bag. She made stuffing and shoved it in as deep as she could, then she sewed the bird up, kissed it right in the belly, and heaved into the oven.

She washed her hands, then went up to look for Meredith again, but she still didn't answer her door. This began to worry Lorraine. On the way back down to her apartment, she wondered what she would do if

Meredith didn't show up. Even if she wanted to, she couldn't invite Roy over now that she'd shoved his birthday gift to her in her cabinet of useless electronics. She rushed back up to Meredith's apartment and tacked a note on her door saying she should come downstairs as soon as she got home.

By four o'clock the smell of turkey had driven Lorraine into a frenzy. There was nowhere in her apartment she could go without smelling it—not her bedroom, not even her bathroom. She hadn't eaten all day and she was starved, her taste buds going wild with anticipation of what the turkey would feel like on her tongue. She walked back and forth in the kitchen, taking deep breaths, and turning the oven light on and off so she could watch the turkey bake.

By 6:30 the temperature gauge had popped up and the bird was done. She took it out of the oven and sat it on top of the stove to cool. She still hadn't heard from Meredith and she was afraid her feast would be completely ruined. Throughout the day, in all the fantasies she'd had about eating this meal, she never once pictured she would be alone. This was not how she planned it. She leaned against the sink and sulked for a minute. Only the sight of the perfect turkey, browned and succulent, could lift her spirits.

She set the table for two, then ran upstairs to Meredith's one more time. But it hit her, as she stood reading the note she'd left on the door, ready to knock one more time anyway: it was the last weekend of the month. Meredith always went to her daughter's in New Jersey on the last weekend of the month. Lorraine was alone, alone with her turkey.

She tramped down the stairs in despair, almost desperate enough to call Roy and beg him to come over. She knew it was short notice, but he was her only son, her only flesh and blood. If she pleaded he'd have to come. If she let him see how weak and pathetic she was, he couldn't refuse.

She'd almost made up her mind to call Roy, but as she passed Mr. Montaigne's door she got another idea. It was a crazy idea, one she would probably regret later, but it seemed like a better idea than baring her soul to Roy. She pressed her ear to the door to see if she could hear anything, but it seemed quiet inside, the TV not even going. She knocked loudly, then stood back; she could feel the blood rushing through the back of her ears. There wasn't a stir inside the apartment, so she knocked again, saying, "Mr. Montaigne! Mr. Montaigne, it's Lorraine Hovington."

Still silence, then she heard footsteps. Suddenly her nervousness turned to fear. She had only seen Mr. Montaigne three times and only spoken to him once. She wasn't even sure if she would recognize him. And what if he did have a tumor bulging from his neck?

The door creaked open, and a white face peered out of the

darkness. "Yes?" Mr. Montaigne said.

"I . . . Hello, Mr. Montaigne." She was stammering like an idiot. She composed herself, cleared her throat, and then in the most soothing voice she could manage, said "I didn't want to bother you, but I've made this turkey, you see, and I've no one to share it with."

He stared at her blankly. She still could only see his face. His head, with his thick crop of tousled white hair, looked as if it were suspended in the doorjamb without a body attached to it. Perhaps, Lorraine thought, his body had grown so hideous due to his illness that he was ashamed for anyone to see it.

"I thought you might be hungry," she said, hoping, praying, her voice didn't sound as coarse as it did on her answering machine.

The door creaked again and Mr. Montaigne took one step into the hallway. Lorraine stepped backward, but she was relieved. There were no visible tumors.

"You want me to have dinner with you?"

"That's the short of it."

Mr. Montaigne scratched his whiskers. He looked as if he hadn't shaved in a few days, but there were smooth spots on his beard where the hair didn't grow. His left eye twitched continually as if he were winking at her in the most grotesque manner. Lorraine could smell cigarette smoke coming from his apartment.

"I don't think so," he said.

"Please, Mr. Montaigne. A good meal will help you sleep."

He looked at her quizzically. "I sleep fine," he said. And then, "I wouldn't want to trouble you. I've got my own dinner."

He probably had no idea she heard him at night, she thought. He probably would be embarrassed if he knew she heard him moaning like he did.

"Please," she said. "It's no trouble at all. I've already got the table set."

Mr. Montaigne took a deep breath, then wheezed a little as the air came out of his body. He stretched his arms into the air, grimaced as if he were in pain, and then yawned.

"Okay," he said.

Back in her apartment, the smell of the turkey intoxicated Lorraine. She decided this was a special occasion and she would like a glass of wine to commemorate it. She had one bottle in the refrigerator for a time just like this, and, after he'd sat down at the kitchen table, she handed Mr.

Montaigne a corkscrew, asking if he would open it for her. He didn't appear up for the task, but must have felt obligated, so he held the bottle between his knees and worked at the cork. When he finally opened the bottle he let out a grunt like a weight lifter who had just overexerted himself. Lorraine jumped at the sound of it and almost dumped her candied yams on the floor. Then Mr. Montaigne said he was hot and asked if he could open the window. Lorraine said that would be fine, though she moved the turkey to the table, lest it catch a chill from the outside air. Mr. Montaigne then yanked up the window and let out another cry that made the hair stand up on Lorraine's arms. She was beginning to think he had a joint problem. He appeared to be in excruciating pain every time he moved.

"Sounds like you're in a lot of pain," she said.

"Ummhmf," Mr. Montaigne grunted.

"Isn't there anything you can do for that?"

"I'm fine," he said.

She didn't want to press him, and the turkey was almost cool enough to eat now, so she busied herself bringing everything else to the table. She handed Mr. Montaigne two wine glasses and asked if he would do the honors. He filled the glasses, drank his, then filled it again.

"Thirsty, aren't we?" she said as she sat down.

She raised her wine glass. "A toast," she said.

"To what?"

"To turkey. To turkey and to children!"

She sipped her wine and he slugged down half his glass.

"To children?" he said. "Why to children?"

"I don't know," she laughed. She thought about telling him about the dream she had, but feared he'd think she was fantasizing about him. "I was just thinking about children today and if I had enough of them. I only had one. Do you have any children?"

"Naw. I almost did once, but took care of that." He coughed and hacked something up into his napkin. Then he smiled and said, "Excuse me. Thank you, Mrs. Hovington, for dinner. This all looks wonderful."

Lorraine smiled. He could be nice if he chose to be. "It is a fine turkey, isn't it?"

"Yes, ma'am. Shall I cut her open?" he said, reaching for the knife.

"No, no, not just yet. I want to know why you never had children."

Mr. Montaigne slouched in his chair. He sighed and rolled his eyes. "Please, Mrs. Hovington, I'd rather just eat."

"Tell me. I want to know. Do you regret it?"

"No, I *don't* regret it. And it wouldn't be any of your business if I did, would it?"

"I'm sorry. I didn't mean to upset you," she said, and she heard the roughness in her voice as it began to go on about the dream she had. "I just, I mean. I had a dream the other night. A funny, silly little dream. You were in it. You and I. I don't know why—we hadn't crossed each other's path in God knows how long. And there you were in this dream, sitting on a porch—I was sitting there, too. I don't know if we were together. Well, we were together there on the porch. And, it's crazy, I know, but there were children playing in the yard."

"Children," Mr. Montaigne said flatly.

"Yes, children. And I got to thinking, wondering, if you had children. I only had the one, you know. I didn't mean to upset you. I was, I was, just—what do you think about this? Do you think it could mean anything?"

"I think it could mean that you are completely, utterly insane."

"Oh," she said, folding her hands across her lap, hanging her head.

"May I carve the turkey now?"

Lorraine stared longingly at the turkey one more time. She was famished by now, but she couldn't bear the thought of seeing the turkey cut open.

"May I?" he prompted her again.

Men were all the same, she thought. They wanted to take something from you. He was no different than Gerald Polario or the Hodgkins man at Louis' Thrift. They all made their demands and expected you to give them what they wanted, regardless of how you felt now or later. She wouldn't give him the satisfaction.

"When you moan in pain like a wounded dog in the middle of the night, Mr. Montaigne, don't you wish you had a son or daughter to call? Don't you wish you weren't so utterly alone that your bones ache every time you turn over in bed?"

Mr. Montaigne pushed his chair back with his legs and slid back from the table. His white face turned near purple. He looked as if he'd stopped breathing. His head bobbed side to side. He looked at Lorraine, then at the table, then back at Lorraine. Then he stood up and he grabbed the turkey with his bare hands.

Lorraine got up in disbelief. "What are you doing? Put it back! Put it back right now!"

But Mr. Montaigne didn't stop. He lumbered over to the window, grunting in pain, then he heaved the turkey out into the night sky with a piercing wail. Lorraine stuck her head outside just in time to see it splatter in the street light below.

She wasn't sure if the next scream came from her or him, but it sounded like *kee-ya* as she threw a right-hand cross against his chin. He fell backward and she hit him again, screaming, "You're a pig! You're a dog! You deserve what you have!"

He fell down and crawled across the floor, yelping like an animal. "Eeee—owww—ughnn." And Lorraine ran after him, kicking him until he made it out the door.

Then she shouted in the hall as he fumbled for the keys to his apartment. "I hope you cry in misery all night, old man. I hope you just die and get it over with."

He got his door unlocked and slammed it behind him, leaving her alone in the hall, listening to him lock and chain himself in his apartment.

*   *   *

She calmed herself by sipping on her glass of wine. She spilled some of it on her blouse, though, her hands were shaking so badly. She sat on the windowsill, rocking back and forth, occasionally looking down at the mess on the sidewalk, shivering from the wind.

Finally, she shut the window and ate some cold candied yams. They soothed her throat, which hurt from screaming, and she thought she may have found the secret to softening her voice. So, she picked up the phone and dialed Roy's number. His answering machine picked up and she disconnected the line before it could begin recording.

She put the phone back, but then dialed the number again, and when the machine began recording she said: "Roy, this is your mother. I had a little accident today."

She wanted to continue but a wave of soft laughter overcame her and she sat there giggling to the machine. "But, I'm fine. There's no need to worry. I thought I would invite you over for dinner one day this week. Only, I doubt I'll cook. Maybe you should just stop at the Colonel's. Or, better yet, pick up some Chinese, my only son."

You Should See This

My brother, Lawrence, lives in a motel at the foot of the Grand Tetons in Wyoming. Every time he writes he sends me pictures of these huge, snow-capped mountains. "The snow never goes away, even in July when it's hot," he says. He tells me the first thing he does every morning is sit at his balcony window for fifteen minutes, just watching the mountains. I've never understood how he could watch mountains. They don't move, do they? To me, the Tetons look like big, gray chunks of metal. From a distance, in the pictures, it looks as if there aren't even trees on them. "Dizzying," my brother writes. "Absolutely dizzying."

Thank God my sister-in-law, Angela, sends photographs, too (in separate mailings). If it weren't for her, I wouldn't even remember what my brother's family looks like. Angela has one of those fancy cameras with the timers that can take pictures automatically. She sends me these great shots of her, Lawrence, and their daughter, Catherine, in front of the fireplace. Only, you can tell they're always racing to beat the camera. I think it's a competition for them. Each takes their turn setting the timer. In one shot, Lawrence and Catherine are laughing hysterically as they look up at Angela, who hasn't sat down fast enough. Her head is cut off at the top of the picture, and on the back of it she wrote: "Come see the Headless Woman of Wyoming. Admission only $1." In another shot, Catherine is cradled in Angela's arms and they're laughing at Lawrence, who's been quick enough to get his face in the picture, but not the rest of his body. His head looks like it's floating in mid-air, but he's got the biggest smile I've ever seen across his face. The best one, though, is when Catherine beat the camera. Lawrence and Angela are sitting side by side on the floor and Catherine has just dove into their arms, turning her head and smiling just in time for the camera to snap the picture. I think it's the only shot I have where all their body parts are present and accounted for.

I'd been flipping through the pictures after Lawrence called this afternoon, and, for some reason, I shoved them into my coat pocket on the way out the door. Now, standing in Kmart underneath a big, red banner that says "CHRISTMAS BONANZA," I switch the pictures to the pocket on the inside of my coat, where I can feel them against my chest, where I know they can't fall out.

My mind is made up to buy Lawrence a present, though we don't normally exchange gifts. We don't bother with the holidays anymore. One time he called on Thanksgiving and we both sounded real awkward on the phone, leaving these long gaps of silence. Finally, Lawrence said, "This is silly. I don't feel like talking right now. I just called because it was the thing to do. Everybody calls everybody on the holidays. It's silly." I agreed, and we decided we'd only call when we had something to say to one another, which, for us, usually happens once every three or four months.

Lawrence moved to Wyoming six years ago. As long as I can remember, his greatest ambition was to be a forest ranger—but in a real forest, he always said, out West. "The woods of Connecticut aren't real forests. I'm thinking bigger than that," he told me. So, when he landed a job at Grand Teton National Park, I thought to myself, this is a man who has fulfilled the American Dream. Born in a small Connecticut town, the son of a plumber, Lawrence somehow got the notion that he could do whatever he wanted. He was the rebel in my family. I always admired him for that. My father was crushed when Lawrence, the eldest son, refused to become his apprentice. "I want Piedmont Pipes to become a family business," my father told him, "and you want to be like that Dr. Doo-Little character, or whatever his name is, talking to the animals."

"Sorry, you'll have to rely on Jack for your family business."

My father looked at me and winced. "But Lawrence, you're the oldest, you're like the heir."

"This is America, Pop, not sixteenth-century Europe."

My brother, the Heir of Piedmont Pipes, renouncing his throne. It was quite a moment in my family's history. After that came several forestry and wildlife management courses, then he met Angela, and they had Catherine.

*   *   *

Lawrence wasn't sure why he called his brother. He'd never been able to elicit good advice or sympathy from Jack, though, he knew he probably wouldn't invest much in his opinions anyway. Jack is his younger brother, and Lawrence has never been able to see beyond that. He's amazed at how JFK could put so much faith in Bobby Kennedy. Eight years ago, when he first contemplated marrying Angela, Lawrence asked Jack if he thought he should do it, and his younger brother said, "Yeah, she's good-looking."

"But she called me Larry last night," Lawrence said. "I got upset and told her never to call me that. She said she wouldn't do it again, but she sounded facetious. What if she really sees me as a Larry?"

"Lawrence, so what?" Jack said. "Not only is she a looker, but she's willing to go off with you and live in the woods. How many opportunities like this will you have?"

That was back when Lawrence took courses at Piedmont Community College—where he met Angela.

One of his classes met in Greenfield Hall, a dark, musty old building with classrooms in the basement, where the walls were thick concrete, dull and green, and pipes ran the length of the ceilings. Usually the professor let them out early because he disliked the place so much. His classmates wasted no time in leaving, filing out of the room as if the fire alarm had been pulled. But Lawrence liked the quiet and the solitude. He'd stay and study for an hour or two, until the next class came. Sometimes he'd just sit there and think, staring up at the pipes. He'd go for short walks down the hallway to stretch his legs, following the pipes with his eyes. Once, he followed a pipe right into the bathroom, which was fine because he had to go anyway. He unzipped his fly, his eyes still on the pipe, expecting to see it connect with a sink or a toilet, but it just hugged the ceiling and went right through the wall into the next room.

He turned to use one of the urinals, but there were none, only stalls. Then he noticed the woman standing at the sink, holding a hair brush, looking at him with his hand on his zipper.

"Tired of the men's room?" she said.

Lawrence zipped his pants. He could feel his face becoming flush. "My father's a plumber," he said. "I have some sort of fascination with pipes."

"Huh?"

"But I don't want to be a plumber."

She looked at him quizzically for a second, then went back to brushing her hair.

"Sorry," he said, going to the door.

"So, what do you want to be?" she called out after him.

Two weeks later, he brought her home for the first time, to show her some of the jigsaw puzzles he'd collected. He introduced her to Jack. Later, he asked him, "So what do you think of Angela?"

"Real pretty. Where'd you find her?"

∗　　　　　∗　　　　　∗

A disco version of "O Come All Ye Faithful" plays on the sound system. It's interrupted by an advertisement for an antifreeze that's on sale—two dollars off if you send in the rebate. I'm skeptical about all the savings rhetoric that goes on at department stores. I make $16,000 a year and I spend $16,000 a year. If I save fifty cents on razor blades, I spend it on a Snickers bar. There's no savings. It's just a matter of spending less in one place and more in another.

I often wonder if my brother faces the same kind of dilemma out there in the Tetons. I can't imagine the Sunday paper advertisements roping him into Sears for a blender he doesn't need. Sometimes I wish I had followed in his footsteps. Nothing could ever have stopped him. He packed his family and every possession he owned into a U-Haul and drove off into the sunset without a second thought. A week and a half later, he called my mother collect from Wyoming. "This is the top of the world," he said. "The Bighorns, the Tetons, Yellowstone. I'll never regret not banging on pipes. Pipes are just a job, Mom. This is life."

They moved into the motel at the foot of the Tetons. Lawrence was the manager. Two years later, he was a ranger in the park (Angela taking over the motel management), his dream realized. I was happy for him, but jealous. Me, just a teller at Piedmont Savings, saved from plumbing by my ineptitude, but not amounting to much of anything else. Maybe mountains aren't my thing, but at least Lawrence has a "thing." And, when I think about it, Lawrence is probably on the right track, investing so much in those mountains. He's on the side of nature, fighting against Kmart and Coca-Cola. I bet you he'd list that as one of his top ten reasons for leaving Connecticut: too many Kmarts. He's a fighter all right, Lawrence.

∗　　　　　∗　　　　　∗

Angela was in the other room when Lawrence called his brother. Of all people, she didn't know why he called Jack. They may be brothers, she thought, but they're not conversationalists when they're around each other. Lawrence doesn't try to make it any better, either. "Jackie's still a kid," he always says. But if she remembered correctly, Jack was close to twenty-six.

She didn't mean to listen, but it was hard not to in their little apartment attached to the motel. Besides, Lawrence hadn't spoken to her since the night before and, at first, she thought he was losing his mind, talking to himself. Most of the day he had been just sitting there in his chair, working on one of his puzzles. Later, he began to pace the living room, the floorboards creaking as he went back and forth. She could hear him talking about her, laying all the blame on her, she thought.

She wondered what Jack was saying on the other end of the line, unable to imagine him speaking ill of her. Jack didn't say a word the first time they met. She and Lawrence had just finished a date and he was giving her a tour of his parents' house, showing off all the jigsaw puzzles he'd done over the years. She never knew a man could have such patience. That was one of the things that attracted her to him so much early on. He delighted in his collection. He had six puzzles hanging in the hallway by his bedroom.

They'd taken off their shoes because it was raining and they'd tramped through the mud. The soft, white carpet felt good beneath her feet as she walked from puzzle to puzzle. The rug was so thick it seemed to quiet the whole house. There were no cracks and pops each time she took a step like the old motel. You couldn't hear anybody walking. Angela didn't even hear Jack come up the stairs, but at first glance she caught him looking at her breasts. He turned red and walked right past her and Lawrence.

"Jackie, this is Angela," Lawrence said.

"Hey," Jack said, but just kept on going. Lawrence didn't even skip a beat, pointing out to her how the sunlight blended the rocks with the ocean in a picture taken off Cape Cod.

"Nothing like a sunset at Cape Cod," he said. "But that was one of the hardest puzzles I ever did."

Months later, though, Jack would open up to her. He'd talk to her more than he'd talk to his own brother. One time, she stopped by the house to see Lawrence, but he wasn't there. Jack invited her in anyway, saying he expected Lawrence soon. He ushered her into the kitchen and sat her down at the table to wait.

"One second," he said, "I'll be right with you." He climbed up on one of the counters to replace a bulb in the fluorescent light that hugged the ceiling. "My father thinks I can't do anything around the house, thinks I can't do anything mechanical. I've been trying to prove him wrong for years."

He got the bad bulb out and held the new one in his hands, trying to figure out which way it went in. "He's been begging Lawrence to take over the plumbing business since he turned eighteen, but he never even asks me for help. Which is fine because I don't want to be a plumber. I mean, I wish I did. I wish I wanted to be *something*. I don't have Lawrence's vision."

With those words he reached for the light and fell to the kitchen floor. He picked himself up instantly and stomped around the room, bumping into chairs, opening the refrigerator and slamming it shut, emptying the water out of the teapot. His face was swelling red. "Damn, my father. Why do I try to impress him?"

He didn't even realize he couldn't move his arm until Angela noticed his hand just hanging there, limply, and asked him if he was all right. She thought he was going to pass out. She had to hold him up as she led him to her car.

All the way to the hospital he kept muttering, to her, or to himself, Angela wasn't sure. "I wish I just wanted to live in the woods," he said. "Lawrence has it made. He *knows* what he wants. He *knows*. I've got no clue." He pressed his cheek against the window. "He's lucky to have you, too," he said, the words muffled against the glass.

*   *   *

I cut through an aisle loaded with fake Christmas trees. I never understood the Christmas-tree tradition and I haven't had one since I moved out of my parents' house. I wonder if Lawrence ever got one for his family in Wyoming. I imagine him trudging through deep snow out in the wilderness, ax in hand, searching for the right tree. I can't imagine anyone in Wyoming driving to Kmart, picking out one of these blue Christmas trees with gold garland, and shoving it into the back of a Bronco II. What would Kmart be like in Wyoming? "Attention, Wyoming shoppers. Take advantage of our blue Christmas tree special—today only. Why bother with nature when you can buy artificial? Fire-retardant trees with a five year guarantee on sale now."

The next time my brother calls, I'm going to ask him how far you'd have to drive from the Tetons to find a Kmart. Or, maybe not the next time. That may be inappropriate considering recent developments. I tend to be insensitive during some of our conversations—like when he called earlier today. He was really quiet. I felt funny standing there holding the phone without saying anything, so I started rambling on about myself and what was wrong with my life.

"You're so lucky," I said to him at one point. "Not only do you want to do something, you're doing it. I'll never leave Piedmont. I'll probably never leave the bank. I wouldn't know where to go or what to do. I wish I had a vision like you. How do you get a vision, Lawrence?"

He was quiet for a minute, and I figured the question was unanswerable. Visions could not be developed. They were inherent and only a select number of people had them. The rest of us were stuck working as bank tellers, or plumbers, or at department stores. I was about to change the subject and ask him if there was much snow in Wyoming, when my brother cleared his throat and said: "Angela is leaving me. She's taking Catherine."

There was one of those gaps of silence, then Lawrence said, "She hates Wyoming."

"Oh," I said. I said it to myself, really, for now I knew why he called. There's always a reason.

"She's going to San Francisco."

"California? With the traffic and the pollution and the gangs? She'll be sorry."

"California is big. There are nice places. Yosemite is nice. Someday I might like to transfer there."

"Well, couldn't you do it now and go with her?"

"She wants to live in the city, close to the coast. She wants to be able to take Catherine to a real movie theater. I can't leave here."

It never occurred to me that there might not be a real movie theater in the Grand Tetons.

"That's all," Lawrence said. "Tell mom I said hi. I'll write her about this later. Take care of yourself."

Take care of myself. Not in my twenty-six years had my brother ever told me to "take care of myself." It's not the kind of thing we say to each other. He already sounded lonely. I imagined him sitting there in a hard, wooden chair, staring out at his mountains, moping for days on end.

"You, too," I said. I held the phone quietly to my ear for another few seconds. Finally there was a click and I was disconnected from Wyoming.

*   *   *

Lawrence got off the phone with Jackie and sat down at his work area. He's been doing the same puzzle for two months now, mostly because he hasn't had much free time. The scene is from Monument Valley, Arizona. The entire foreground is made up of sand and green cacti plants. It's one of those puzzles where there's no distinct object to focus on, no place to build from, so it takes forever. Plus, he's been getting headaches every time he works on it. He thinks he may need glasses. Angela made her announcement last night and he took the day off from work, trying to bury himself in the puzzle, but his concentration was completely broken.

She had been packing all day, confining herself mostly to the bedroom, but, every now and then, gathering things from the living room. Several times she paused by his work space, and he felt her looking over his shoulder at his hands fiddling with the puzzle pieces. He could tell she wanted him to speak to her, but he had nothing to say. He'd keep looking down at the puzzle, or he'd look out toward the mountains, though he couldn't see anything because three quarters of the window was frozen over.

Shortly after he got off the phone, she came into the living room, keeping her distance this time. She sat down on the musty, old trunk that served as a coffee table in the middle of the room. They'd brought it all the way from Lawrence's attic in Connecticut. His grandfather said he'd used it to carry cymbals when he was the director of a marching band in the 1950s. Lawrence said they would need it for storage space, but to this day it was empty. From time to time, they would clear it off and Catherine would use it as a stage, putting on pretend singing concerts for her parents. She'd stand on top of it with her shiny black shoes, holding a play microphone beneath her chin, singing along to recordings of Gloria Estefan or Madonna. Lawrence thought it was ridiculous for a seven-year-old to sing "Like a Virgin," but Angela loved it and clapped wildly while Catherine bowed again and again.

Now, his wife was leaving him and she sat there on the trunk, crinkling the latest copy of *National Parks*, which he hadn't read yet.

"How's Jack?" she said.

"I don't know." Lawrence kept his back turned, his fingers digging through puzzle pieces without purpose.

"He never did come out here to visit. You should have invited him. I could have taken him to Jackson Hole. Shown him how to ski."

"Catherine has been at Natalie's all day. I don't think you should leave her there alone much longer."

Lawrence faced her now. She sat silently for a few seconds, looking at him, as if she were trying to draw something out of him with her eyes. But he felt like stone inside—cement, still hardening. Soon it would be too late to crack through it. He didn't know what she wanted from him. He would have preferred to have come home to an empty house with a note on the kitchen table. Why couldn't she have said she was going to leave and then left? Lawrence thought the cruelest part was that she stayed around for a whole day, packing, as if to give him an opportunity to stop her.

"I'm almost finished," she said quietly. Then she stood up slowly and went back into the bedroom.

*   *   *

Finally, I reach my destination—the toy and hobby section. I came here to get Lawrence something that will relax him, something that will say, "I'm sorry about Angela and all, take care of yourself." The only gift I can think of to do the job is a jigsaw puzzle. When Lawrence was young, he'd spend hours in his room quietly doing puzzles. Sometimes, my parents and I wouldn't call him for dinner because we thought he wasn't home. Usually he worked on puzzles that depicted nature scenes—a rickety boat along the shore, wheat fields with old gray shacks. There always had to be something old and worn-out in it to catch Lawrence's interest. Each time he finished a puzzle he'd glue the pieces together, frame it, and put it up on a wall, or give it to someone. Sometimes I'd see him standing there, his hands clasped in front of him, staring at one of his puzzles up on the wall in his room. He seemed to meditate on them. Lawrence always was so serene.

When I find them, I can see my work is cut out for me. Half an aisle is filled with all kinds of puzzles—Disney stuff, hot air balloons, an open refrigerator stuffed with junk food, four puppies sitting on the back of a pick-up truck—but not many good nature scenes. Of course, what I really want is a nice shot of the Grand Tetons in 3000 pieces. That would be ideal.

As I wade through the boxes, a kid comes up behind me and starts crowding me, looking at the same puzzles as me. I can hear her steadily breathing through her mouth. I keep waiting to smell her breath or feel it on the back of my neck. She's tall for a kid. Finally, she steps in front of me and grabs a puzzle—a picture of candy apples, caramel corn, and cotton candy all bunched together. She holds it in front of her for a few seconds, then puts it back.

"Too easy," she says. "Some of these puzzles are way easy. I'm real good at 'em."

I take a few steps away from her, to discourage conversation. Her heavy breathing returns as we browse for another minute. Then she says, "But I love puzzles. I sure do."

I look at her and smile a little fake smile. I can't relate. I've never done a jigsaw puzzle.

She picks up a couple other puzzles, looks them over, shakes them and puts them back. "I can't help but smile to myself when I put in that last piece of the puzzle. I never let anybody help me. I do it all myself. Do you?"

I hate to be rude. And it was a direct address, so I say, "No." Then, I look at her for the first time. She doesn't look like the type of kid who sits quietly in a room and does puzzles. Her hair is greasy and disheveled. An old, maroon-colored, down coat, with a slit in its sleeve, sags loosely off her shoulders. A feather or two puff out into the air each time she moves. She's wearing a white T-shirt that's too small, with red pants that are too long and too tight, unbuttoned just below her navel. I can see her navel. How can a kid who was taught so little hygienic discipline learn the patience to build puzzles by herself? I used to think puzzle-building was strictly for clean-cut people—people like Lawrence, who got straight A's in school, or maybe played clarinet in the band.

Her breathing grows louder as she looks at me, as if she was expecting me to say more. I quickly turn back to the shelf and keep digging through the pile of puzzles. She does the same. Way in back, buried behind all the other boxes, I find a couple things that are closer to what I'm looking for—a desert picture from New Mexico, and a picture of a lake in Switzerland. But still, no Tetons or anything like them.

I feel the kid looking over my shoulder during all this, trying to get a glimpse of the puzzles I'm interested in without being that obvious. I put Switzerland and New Mexico back and continue to look when I hear: "This is it."

The kid is standing there, money already in hand, a puzzle pressed against her chest like a Teddy bear. She lowers it and looks down at it happily, squeezing it in her hands. I can't help but be nosey. I owe it to her. It's a picture of mountains of some sort. When I look more closely I see that it's 3,000 pieces—what I want. And then I see the little print on the corner of the box by her thumb: YOSEMITE NATIONAL PARK.

It's the next best thing to the Grand Tetons. Lawrence said he wanted to transfer there some day.

The kid looks over at me, her face glowing, as if she can sense she has something I want. "Bye," she says, starting to walk away.

"Hey, wait," I say. I'm actually going to try to reason with her. "Did you see these here? Wouldn't you rather a picture of the desert, or Switzerland?"

"No." She tries walking away again, so I follow her.

"I'll give you five bucks if you don't buy that puzzle," I say.

"No," she says again.

"Ten. Ten dollars, plus I'll buy you any other puzzle you want." I don't want her to be able to refuse.

She presses the Yosemite puzzle against her chest for a second, as if she's mulling over my proposal, but I begin to think this was her plan all along—to get whatever she could out of me.

"Okay," she says and hands me the puzzle.

Then, she sits on the floor in front of the shelves and starts searching all over again. I check my wallet and find I only have twelve dollars. I'll have to give her ten and put our puzzles on my credit card. We'll have to go out together.

Finally, she settles for the New Mexico desert picture and I follow her to the cash register, feathers coming out of her jacket as she walks. The lines are long, but someone opens up another register as soon as we get there. Several people rush in front of us, forming a new line, the kid and I bringing up the rear. She holds the puzzle gently in front of her and, I think to myself, what a strange thing this is to have such an obsession with puzzles. It's not normal.

Another thought follows that one: what if puzzle-making is hereditary? What if Lawrence's daughter, Catherine, has it in her blood? She'd be destined to build puzzles, but with a good family life she'd turn out okay. What if Lawrence and Angela's divorce jolted her so much psychologically that she turned out like this kid, unbuttoned pants, greasy hair, talking to strangers in department stores? Angela will get through it okay. She wants to be separated. Lawrence will mope, maybe for a couple years, but he'll get through it. But Catherine?

"I hate waiting," the kid says, shaking the puzzle.

"Me, too," I say, hoping the line would move fast so I won't have to talk to her anymore. I don't even want to look at her. All I can see is Catherine's face from the pictures Angela's sent, blended in with that ripped down coat, feathers falling out. For the first time, it occurs to me that I have to live with the fact that my brother has reproduced. He's made a family and now he's screwing it up. And I'm the God-parent.

As we stand there quietly, I have to listen to the kid breathe, so I'm not sure if silence is better. I'm relieved when she says, "The people who work at this store are always slow."

"Yeah? I don't come here much." And I don't talk to kids much. I don't know how to have a conversation with one, so I stand there, stupidly, listening to her breathe some more.

Finally, I hold the puzzle out in front of me and stare at it. I never knew what Yosemite looked like. This puzzle here is a winter scene. In the foreground are snow-coated trees lined up alongside a glassy stream that reflects the rest of the picture. And there are mountains all right, but not like the Tetons. These are just huge chunks of rock. That's all they look like—big, egg-shaped rocks, with ice and snow crusted across them. They look impossible to climb. They look lifeless. Even those weird goats that have two legs shorter than the others, enabling them to adapt to the mountains they live on, couldn't survive here. I can't even see trees, at first. But then I look closer and I see them. Seven, maybe eight trees are scattered throughout this one mountain. They're growing straight out of the rock, shooting into the air at forty-five degree angles. It's the weirdest thing I've ever seen. Then, I look even closer and I can see the trees have a blue tinge to them. Blue, like those fake Kmart Christmas trees.

The kid is looking at my puzzle now, too. "It's a nice picture," she says. "But it's not real. I mean, it's a real picture, but they add to it. They touch it up to make it look better."

I drop the puzzle on the conveyor belt by the register; the pieces slide back and forth. Fake, blue trees sticking out of a mountain. Kmart has infiltrated nature, I think to myself. How will Lawrence take this? He's giving up his family for artificial trees. Right then it hits me. I've got to speak to him as soon as possible. I've got to tell him: nature's losing the battle. Give up the fight, Lawrence, and keep what you've got.

The line in front of us has dissipated and the puzzles move down the conveyor belt until the clerk rings them up. "Good deal on these puzzles," he says. "Save some money there."

"I really don't think I'm saving that much. I don't think I'm saving that much at all," I say.

He looks at me kind of dumfounded and hands me the credit card slip to sign. I sign it and then me and the kid are gone. Out in the parking lot, she says, "Those people are so slow in there."

"They're worse than slow," I say.

"Sometimes I just don't know what to do with 'em."

"There's nothin' you can do. Just wait and hope you can enjoy life for a while before they get ya to buy one of those fake, blue Christmas trees."

"Huh?" the kid says. She's reaching into the bag, trying to grab her puzzle.

"Keep 'em both," I say and hand her the bag.

"You don't want yours?"

"Naw."

"Well, you can keep your ten bucks then."

"No," I say, getting my money out of my wallet. "You take it." I hand her the ten and both ones.

"Thanks," she says.

"Take care," I say. She's trying to shove the money in her pocket, but she can't because her pants are too tight, and I'm off, running to my car, trying to get home and call Lawrence as fast as I can, thinking how ridiculous that must have sounded to tell a twelve-year-old kid to take care of herself.

*   *   *

The station wagon was packed, so much so that Angela only saw black in the rear-view mirror. Only Catherine's tape recorder was left—the one thing Lawrence would have to give up. She hadn't taken it yet because he was playing his "I Like Myself Unconditionally" cassettes, with ocean sounds in the background, while he worked on his puzzle. That'd be the last thing. She'd keep it in front, between her and Catherine while she drove, because the wagon's radio was broken. Lawrence could *have* whatever else she left behind. She'd make no arguments.

She started the car and gently gave the engine gas until she thought it would idle on its own. Then, leaving her gloves on the front seat, she went back to the motel. The door to the apartment had shut while she was gone, on its own, or by Lawrence, thinking she was gone for good. It was locked and she rapped her fist against it, angry that she'd have to go back to the car for the keys. But then she remembered she'd put the spare key in her pocket, taken it with her as if she might come back some day. She didn't know why. She was never coming back here. She turned the key and shoved the door open, slipping as her snow-covered shoe hit the polished wooden floor. She held onto the doorknob to keep her balance and, aggravated, she looked for Lawrence, to snap at him, to snatch up the tape recorder with his cassette still in it, throw it at him, and leave, screaming at him.

And there he stood, in the center of the living room, atop the old cymbal trunk, Catherine's play microphone in his hand beneath his chin. "Like a virgin," he cried out, literally crying, tears rolling down his face; she could see them from the door. "Touched for the very first time." His voice was cracking as if he would lose it any word now and he did, or he stopped, the microphone hanging by his side. There was no music, and the apartment was silent, except for the muffled chug of the wagon's engine as it struggled to keep running out front.

"Angela, don't leave me," he said, almost whispered.

"Keep the tape recorder," she said, slamming the door behind her.

The car stalled and she paused for a moment, looking up into the darkening sky, listening to the quiet. "You might be my lucky star!" she heard Lawrence shouting from the motel, his voice rough, breaking apart as she started the car and ran the engine full throttle, its whine drowning it out.

*   *   *

It takes forever to dial all those numbers and then the phone keeps ringing and ringing. I haven't even taken off my coat. I slip the photographs out of my pocket and flip through them again. I stop on a picture that Angela took when they last visited Connecticut a few years ago. Catherine and I are in the bathroom—just the two of us. She's about four years old. The lid to the toilet is down and she's standing on top of it. I'm combing her hair. It's long and blonde, clean, her bangs falling to the middle of her forehead.

Lawrence finally answers the phone.

"Lawrence?" I say. "Lawrence, you've got to think about what you're doing here."

"Jackie? That you?"

"I know you love the Tetons, Lawrence, but Angela—she's a living, breathing, human. I mean, a person, Lawrence. And Catherine—she's your kid. Think of her, Lawrence. I'm thinking of her. You can't just let them go."

"It's too late." He sounds out of breath. I can tell he's moving around.

"Lawrence, the mountains, they're losing. I know. I've seen it. Connecticut is crawling with fake trees. And those puzzles—they're mass-producing them. Kmart is dismantling Yosemite into thousands of pieces and then putting it back together—its way, not yours, not ours. We can't win this fight. Give up the vision."

"I told you," he says. He's speaking slowly, softly. He's hoarse, as if he'd been screaming and now he was losing his voice. "It's too late. I was too late."

"I always admired you for what you were doing, Lawrence. Envied you, even. But you're being real pigheaded here. Your priorities are screwed up. I'm telling you. Cut your loses while you can and keep what you've got."

"Jackie, you don't understand. She's out the door. Angela is gone." He goes into a coughing fit; it's so loud I have to hold the phone away from my head.

"Lawrence. Lawrence!"

Finally, he calms down and takes a deep breath. "She left fifteen minutes ago. She's not coming back."

"You let her go? You just let her go? Damn you, Lawrence."

"I tried, but I was too late. I really tried. She's not coming back, ever."

I sit down on the kitchen floor, the phone still to me ear, not saying anything. Lawrence is quiet for a minute, too. But the silence isn't like it usually is between us. It isn't awkward.

"What are you gonna do?" I ask.

"I think I'm going to go for a walk," he says. "It's nice out. I'm standing here on top of Grandpa's big trunk—you know, the thing he said he used to carry cymbals around in? I can see out the window from here. It's mostly iced from the bottom up, but from here I can see outside. The sun's set and there's this orange tinge of light hovering there in the darkness, behind the mountains."

"Lawrence, you okay?" I say, but he keeps on talking. I don't even think he hears me.

"It's nice out. I'm going to go for a walk. You should come out here sometime, Jackie. You should see this."

One Prime Piece of Real Estate

The Realtor—a tall, lanky woman named Peggy, with flaming orange hair teased so high it brushed against the ceiling of the Cadillac—had taken them to two other neighborhoods this morning and both of them had the same feel as this one: too transient. Too many townhomes and slick condominiums nearby with private health spas and swimming pools. They seemed like temporary residences to Abby. The people she saw walking down the street or getting into their cars looked as if they hadn't lived there for more than a year and would be gone within three. This was not what she wanted.

She looked to Ned for affirmation, but he was staring straight ahead at the road, feeling ridiculous because he was sitting in the front seat between the two women. He just as easily could have looked out the back windows, but Abby said he would have a better view from the front and he didn't want to start an argument, not now. Abby had been caressing his thigh nervously, but now she stopped and he felt her fingernails jabbing through his pants. She stared at him with a look that fell somewhere between disgust and sadness—he could never tell which—and when he didn't say anything she rolled her eyes. Finally, as the Realtor was pulling in front of another townhome, Abby leaned across him and said:

"Peggy, this isn't exactly what we were looking for. We were looking for something a little older. Something we could put some work into. Something we could make our own."

The Realtor put the car in park and let the engine idle. "A project home?" she said. A smirk came across her. "You want to put some work into it?" She grabbed Ned's hand and flipped it palm side up.

"This is not a home-builder's hand," she laughed. "Are you sure I can't get you to reconsider, Mrs. Chapdelaigne?"

Ned squirmed in the front seat. He had no defense for such an accusation. In one of the few moments of levity before they went into therapy together during their second year of marriage, he'd asked Abby why she'd married him at all and she'd said: "I married you for your hands. You have the softest, most gentle hands of any man I know."

He was pretty sure she'd meant that as a compliment, but the comment had emasculated him somewhat at the time and, a month later, when he tried to refurbish an old dresser, he purposely scraped his hands against sandpaper, trying to toughen them up. For a day or two they did become very dry and tight, and Ned had initiated lovemaking with Abby twice during this time, taking extra care to caress her all over with his new, rough hands. But he never knew if she noticed or not, and soon his hands were back to their normal womanly state.

Unlike his father, who had had a workbench in the basement with real sawdust, who made wooden cabinets and chests, and things from metal, and rebuilt their garage after it burned down, Ned's most rigorous activity as he grew up had been participating on the golf team at Brown. He remembered having a blister on a finger once, and it cost him a potential eagle on the back nine as he shanked a chip over the green. He'd never had the hands of a workman and he felt completely inadequate for home repair. His father, however, had left them the money in his will for a house, and Abby wanted it. She saw it as their best last chance to put something permanent beneath their feet, something they couldn't easily walk away from.

"We really want something a little older, with more character to it," Abby said, looking again to Ned for support.

"Yeah. We're not afraid of a little hard work," Ned said unconvincingly. "I mean, we don't need to completely rebuild anything, but we'd like to put our stamp on something. I'm sure I can work up some calluses just as well as the next guy."

"We're going to take a home improvement course," said Abby.

"I just want to make sure you've thought about what you want," the Realtor said. "I'd hate to see you jump into something that would turn out to be a total disaster for you."

"We've thought. We know," Abby said. "Who are you to question what we want? You're just the frickin' real estate agent for God's sake."

Ned had not heard the engine running before, but with the silence that filled the car now he could hear a fan belt squeaking and the sound grated on him. The whole situation grated on him.

He felt as if something heavy was about to land on top of him. The sound of the engine reminded him of lying underneath a car during his childhood, watching his father's dirty, dried-up hands grab onto a frozen muffler pipe in February, in New Hampshire. "I need another clamp," his father was saying, but it didn't register with Ned, who was too preoccupied waiting for the Monte Carlo to come crashing down on both of their chests and wondering how his father could be touching metal in ten-degree weather without wearing gloves. He'd always felt both admiration and concern for his father. His father was a motivated man, and nothing—not snow, not ice, not an incompetent son—could stop him from making pipes fit together underneath a car in winter, or repairing a roof in a rainstorm. But Ned always feared his father's death would be a gory event. He'd be trapped underneath a Ford Mustang, falling off a ladder three stories up, or electrocuted at the base of a fifteen-foot TV antenna. In the end, though, he died in his sleep without a sound.

Ned had come to terms with his father's death as well as he had come to terms with the deaths of other members of his family. The repercussions of his father's passing, however, still lingered over Ned's life, namely with a bank check earmarked for a down payment on a house. He couldn't help but feel a little bitter and a little controlled, listening to the Cadillac's squeaking fan belt. If he were not sitting between his wife and the Realtor, he would have quietly slipped out of the car and walked away. He would have resigned his new university appointment in Baltimore and walked all the way back to New Hampshire if he could have. But now he felt it was his duty to fill the silence and restore even the smallest amount of comfort to the car.

He was about to apologize to the Realtor—apologize for hiring her for the excruciating task of carting the two of them around while they bickered and fought over what type of life they wanted together, or if they wanted a life together.

But before Ned could process the right words, Abby was saying, "We're sorry, Peggy. House hunting is just very stressful for us. I'm sure it is for everyone."

"Well, I can take you closer into the city," the Realtor offered. "There are older neighborhoods there. But then you're talking more money, more traffic—but it's up to you."

Finally, they chose a big Victorian on a quiet street that went up a hill leading into a cul-de-sac. Ned was apprehensive about living on a dead-end street; he wanted at least two easy exits from his house. But Abby seemed to have a revelatory experience while standing on the curb, staring up at the pigeons perched on one of the gutters.

"This is it," she said. "I can feel it. I have a vision for it."

"Feel what?" He'd walked up onto the porch and didn't feel anything but nausea from the car ride. The porch seemed to slope to the left, which added to his uneasiness. He felt vertigo coming on. In the front yard there were the same kind of red berry bushes that had been outside his parents' old house. During the summer before he'd entered kindergarten, he'd set himself a goal of picking all the berries off the bushes before school started. But he got tired of it after a week and, instead, tried eating them. He vomited on and off for two days afterward, and his parents had the bushes unearthed.

He didn't even know what these poison bushes were called, but there they were, sitting in the front yard of a house Abby had a vision for while the Realtor fumbled around with her keys, yakking about how the sun stayed in the front yard all day long and it would be perfect for a flower garden.

"You'll love it, Mrs. Chapdelaigne," she was saying. "You can have a bed of tulips right here off the porch."

"Where? In the shade of the pine tree?" Ned said.

"Oh, it's only one tree," the Realtor said and the lock clicked and the door swung open.

Ned stepped inside and the disorienting feeling that he was falling to his left continued straight into the living room.

There were hardwood floors that needed to be completely redone. They were probably beautiful at one point, but now they were hacked and stained. An uneven line had been gouged across the floor from the kitchen to the front door, as if the previous tenants had left in a hurry, dragging things behind them

"It's a bank repossession, Mr. Chapdelaigne," the Realtor said. "Plenty of work for you to do."

Abby had gone straight upstairs. Ned could hear her as she walked excitedly from one room to another. Her feet sounded like hooves against the hard, wooden floors. He heard her say, "Ooooh," and then, suddenly, there was silence.

She had stopped in the bathroom and looked out the window at the backyard. An old garage sat there, with peeling paint and rickety, old doors that you needed to swing open manually on hinges. It was a large garage. Abby surmised it could fit two cars at a minimum. Better yet, it was two stories high and there appeared to be a studio of some sort on the second floor. It even had windows. What caught her eye most, though, was a red door on the outside wall of the second level, twenty-five feet or so from the ground, with nothing below it—no steps, no walkway, no ladder, just air. It baffled her, but intrigued her. They must have used it at some point, but now the entrance to the second-floor loft was on the other side of the garage and that old, red door just remained there in the front of the structure, knob and all.

She sped down the stairs, passing Ned along the way. "It's exactly what I'm looking for!" she said.

She ran out the front of the house, around to the back, and up the stairs to the door that now led into the loft. It was unlocked; with a good shove it opened and she was inside. There was an old wood-burning stove, a chewed-up desk, and a heavy steel bed frame. It would be perfect as a guest house, an office, or a studio. She could take up her drawing again, or continue with her calligraphy. She was an excellent calligraphist. She'd made all of their wedding invitations by hand. This would be the perfect place to renew her talent. It would be an escape and a respite for her or Ned when, and if, they had children. She envisioned Ned going out to the studio for the evening and reading his books, and after the kids were asleep she'd grab a bottle of wine and sneak out there. They could make love as loud as they wanted. This place had so much potential.

"What a shithole," Ned said. He'd come up and stood behind her now. "Goodness, it smells like sewage."

"No," Abby said, "It's just a little musty."

"Musty with dead things laying around somewhere. Dead animal carcasses."

"No, Ned. I really like it. I can see us here."

Ned knew what that meant. She meant she could see them there when they were old and graying, when they had no desire to leave the house, when their most profound activity would be deciding what to watch on the tube.

He had to hand it Abby. She still tried her best to come up with a long-term plan that would keep them together. When he brooded over why he loved her, or whether he was even in love with her at all anymore, or why he should love her, he thought about her determination. When he would have opted for divorce, she chose therapy. When he would have opted for separation, she chose to buy a house. Now she had chosen this particular house, and he would go along with it. He felt he owed her that. She had this fifty-year plan for them that she stuck to despite everything. It was admirable. He wished he had half her stamina. He wished he had her vision, but beyond a week or two, he could see nothing. It had always been like that for him. The future was blank, white space, as nondescript as it could be.

*   *   *

Two days after they moved in, Abby came home with a course catalog from a local community college. She'd left it on the kitchen table where Ned would find it and circled a listing for a class entitled "Home Improvement 101: Making the Most of Your Real Estate." It met every Sunday afternoon at 4:00, the "locations to be announced." The instructor's name was Carl Shank.

Ned had originally agreed to enroll in such a class, but now he was apprehensive about it. There was a lot to be done in and around the house, but he thought he could handle it himself. They'd had the floors done professionally before they moved in and already the place was looking much better. There was a lot of painting to be done, but he could do that without some beer-bellied Mr. Fixit directing him over his shoulder. As far as he could see, the most difficult task was going to be repairing the holes in the wall in the master bedroom, and, after much deliberation, Abby convinced him that was reason enough to take the course.

"Plus, it'll be fun," she said. "We'll learn stuff. We'll meet people."

Fun might have been too strong of a word for Ned, but he conceded that it would be a good opportunity for Abby to meet people in the area. After they enrolled in the class, he admitted that if it were not for Carl Shank, the classes might actually have been enjoyable.

To Ned, Carl Shank was not the sort of person you let into your home. But due to the nature of the class it was unavoidable. Home Improvement 101 was like a round-robin: each week the class met at a different member's house where Carl Shank demonstrated different repair techniques and everyone got some hands-on experience. In that way, the course paid for itself. Each class member got free labor, not to mention know-how. At one couple's house, for example, they put in a new toilet, at another's they worked on the plumbing, at another's they started building a deck.

Inevitably these weekly gatherings became a social event, with food, wine, and beer. Carl Shank contributed a six-pack of Pabst each week and he always made a point of offering one to Ned, who tried to decline respectfully in favor of the cabernet sauvignon. Abby had even befriended some of the other women in the class, meeting them for lunch on a couple of occasions. Ned was less personable with the group, allowing his insecurities to get the best of him when they actually got to working on a project. Once, however, Carl Shank had extended an invitation to Ned and the other men to go to the "the track," as he referred to it. Ned declined publicly on the grounds that he was allergic to animals and feared the horses would get the better of him; privately, however, he didn't want to risk sitting next to Shank, who smelled like a combination of bad body odor and tar—which would have been okay had Shank been a roofer, but as far as Ned knew he was retired. He just taught the class and did odd jobs on the side for a little extra money.

Eventually the week came when the Chapdelaignes' house became Home Improvement 101's "classroom." Abby was in a frenzy on Saturday, the day before the class. She saw this as their first big social occasion, their first time entertaining in their new home. Despite Ned's pleas not to make a big fuss, she went all out, as if she were planning for a gathering of their closest friends, which it occurred to her these people were since she and Ned hadn't met anyone else in Baltimore besides some stuffy university faculty.

She was excited about cooking again. In Manchester, she'd run a catering service and she felt, with the exception of Ned, she could make a human connection with anyone through food. Ned ate like a bird—bland foods with little vibrancy to them, like oatmeal and pea soup. The only type of green he would eat in his salad was iceberg lettuce. It infuriated her sometimes. "Try romaine," she'd say. "Try cabbage, try spinach!"

"No. Thank you," he would say, then quietly stuff a forkful in his mouth so he wouldn't have to respond anymore.

It disheartened her that she couldn't please her own husband on a food level, and sometimes it made her feel inadequate, as if she couldn't satisfy him at all.

But she was damned if she was going to let him spoil the first social occasion in their new home. Her kitchenware hadn't been completely unpacked yet, but she was able to put together a lovely pasta salad with green and orange tortellini, chicken, red peppers, onions, artichoke hearts. It was beautiful, colorful, even Ned would have to admit so much. Then she made hors d'oeuvres of bacon and cheese wrapped around water chestnuts. She went to the grocery store and got fresh vegetables, potato chips, pita bread, and hummus, and she made a dip with crab meat. Then she bought three pies—one cherry, one rhubarb, and one blueberry, and she whipped up some fresh cream until it was airy and weightless. Ned would definitely say she was overdoing it, but she didn't care. At least she would have people over who enjoyed food. This was her chance to show off a little, to regain some of the identity she'd left back in New Hampshire. No doubt, her new friends would be impressed. They'd want to come over for dinner more often. She'd have a regular audience. Ned could eat his lousy iceberg lettuce then sit upstairs by himself all night while she and her friends drank cappuccino and sampled luscious desserts.

After she'd finished preparing the food, she went up to the bedroom where the plastering was to take place. There were two big holes in the wall there—Lord knows what the previous owner had done—one right in the middle of the room, the other just above the floor in the closet. She took as much of the clothes out of the closet as she cared to, then shoved the rest to one side and kicked Ned's shoes out of the way so there would be room to work. She changed the sheets on the bed, tidied the bedspread, and fluffed the pillows, as if they weren't going to sleep on it before the next afternoon. She supposed it didn't matter, though. There wasn't much chance of the bed being ruffled overnight. They had not made love since they moved into the house. Ned had tried twice, but his hands were chapped and he kept scraping them up and down her back until she couldn't stand it anymore. She resorted to saying, "No, not now. Not yet. I just need a little bit of time to settle into my surroundings." Ned would leave her alone, then quietly roll over and go to sleep, and Abby would drape her arm around him, thinking that she hadn't completely lied. She wasn't used to living in the house yet. She'd become disoriented at times, waking up in the middle of the night, tripping around in the dark because she couldn't find the bathroom. It was taking longer for her vision of how things would be once they moved into their own home to come to fruition. She thought it had to do with all the unpacked boxes that still lay around, which made it feel like it would be too easy to pick up and leave before they set down their roots.

When she finished in the bedroom, it was only about five o'clock Saturday evening, still nearly twenty-four hours before the class. She decided she'd do some work on the living room. The more she could do before guests came, the better. She and Ned had divided up some of the home improvement tasks that needed to be done. Besides the loft above the garage, where she spent much of her time, she'd been working mostly in the living room, staining the wood trim and painting the window panes. Ned was in charge of redoing all the doors in the house, which were a mess. She had grown increasingly annoyed at his lethargy and begged him to at least finish the upstairs bathroom door—which he'd removed and brought to the basement—and return it. She knew there was only the two of them, but she felt like the whole world was watching whenever she sat down on the toilet.

With Abby's prompting, Ned had gone down into the basement to work on the doors. He'd removed most of them, giving the house an open, airy feel, which he liked. It made the place look even bigger. Nearly every door in the house had to be stripped and repainted for one reason or another. The door to the upstairs bathroom had been painted an unsettling blood red like the aberrant, red door on the garage; the doors on the first floor were painted an equally unsettling battleship gray. Until he removed them, Ned felt like he was in the navy whenever he ate in the kitchen. The doors to the bedrooms were varnished, but they were chipped and scratched and marked with crayon drawings of animals and people. Abby called them the graffiti doors, and occasionally she had added to the drawings herself despite Ned's pleas not to add to the defacement.

One by one, he'd taken the doors off their hinges and brought them down to the cellar. One at time, he'd lay them across some wooden horses he'd found and begin sanding them, first with coarse sandpaper wrapped around a wooden block, and then with a fine grade that smoothed over the scratches made by the other paper. He'd seen how to do this on PBS, but he had no idea it would take so long just to revamp one door. He struggled at first, not so much with the physical work, but with trying to contain his thoughts—they drifted everywhere from old girlfriends to whether or not he'd made the right career decisions to anxiety over being a homeowner and everything that went with it, including the children that Abby inevitably would want, sooner rather than later, which he didn't know if he wanted in the first place.

When his thoughts wandered, he tried to remain focused on the doors and block everything else out. He told himself that nothing was more important than the short term. Nothing was more important than the doors. Nothing else mattered than how they would look when he finally put them back up.

When Abby called out to him, asking if he was hungry, he shouted up to the ceiling, "No. I am the door man! I am working on the doors! There is no time to eat."

"Glad to hear it," Abby retorted.

"I will care for all the doors. All of them."

She ignored his babbling until he went on about how he should find a way to remove the old door from the top-level of the garage. With a swift stamp on the floor, she shouted, "You'll do no such thing!" She loved that door. It added a sense of mystery to the house that she wanted to keep.

"Fine," Ned shouted. "But one day your parents will be staying up there and in the middle of the night one of them's gonna go out the wrong door and take the tumble of his or her life."

"You can paint it if you want to," Abby said from the top of the stairs. "But that door is staying right where it is."

"It looks stupid," Ned muttered down in the basement. "It looks like we're insane."

There was a reason they were working in different parts of the house, he thought. It was important for them to keep out of each other's way during the first weeks after they moved in. They didn't need to add any extra tension. He was glad to be in the basement, even though it gave him the creeps. There was a large, white freezer in the corner. According to the Realtor, the previous owner had been a meat cutter who had kept beef and pork that had not been sold before its expiration date.

"They were major carnivores," the Realtor had said. "The guy never paid a dime for his protein. Every night it was rump roast or pork loin. His family ate well, believe me. He had a couple of big kids."

Ned pictured an old man hacking beef down in the basement every day. There were red spots all over the freezer, but he couldn't tell if they were blood stains or paint. He'd summoned the courage days ago to check the freezer to make sure it was empty, but every so often he had to resist compulsive urges to check it again.

The cellar had been painted haphazardly with, to Ned's best estimation, seven different colors in various places, as if someone had taken out a roller, started with one color, got bored, and switched to another. Half of one wall was purple and peach, the other half orange. Another wall was pale green. The combinations were enough to turn anyone's stomach and he tried to keep looking down at the floor, which, for the most part, was the battleship-gray color of the doors from the first floor. When the time was right, he was going to rent a spray gun and lock himself down in the basement with it until the whole place was repainted. He'd have to pick a dark color, though, one the previous colors wouldn't bleed through—maybe brown, or maroon. Something different, something other than basement gray.

He continued sanding the red bathroom door. Fine, red dust rose up through the air giving the basement an added sense of the surreal. He'd been wearing a protective mask over his nose and mouth, and by now the white mask had turned red, along with his arms and shirt and hair. He got into a rhythm, sanding with the grain until he thought the door was ready to be primed. He brushed the dust off with his hands. The wood was smooth, still warm from the friction. Lines of red dust were packed underneath his fingernails and his hands were tight and dry. They were getting callused and he felt proud. He felt different about himself, as if he were temporarily occupying another body. He felt adventurous, a little aroused. He began to fantasize about Abby and thought he might even go upstairs and make a pass at her—make a pass at his own wife. He imagined her being hesitant at first, reluctant, telling him he needed a shower, laughing at him as he stood there with the mask over his face. But he'd seduce her, and before he took her clothes off his red hand prints would be all over her blouse and blue jeans, and they'd make red, dusty love right there on their brand-new hardwood floors. He imagined her saying, "You feel different. Your hands. Everything."

His fantasy ended with the sound of a second set of footsteps upstairs—loud, heavy footsteps that made the floor crackle and ping. His first reaction was to panic for fear that someone had broken into the house. He tripped over one of the wooden horses that supported a door. The whole thing came down with a crash. He stopped to see if there would be any reaction from upstairs, but there wasn't. He could hear Abby having a conversation with someone. She didn't sound threatened.

Nonetheless, Ned quietly inched his way up the stairs. The cellar door was halfway open and he peered around the corner. Carl Shank stood in the living room, one hand on Abby's shoulder, the other pointing up at the ceiling.

"Right along here," he was saying. "From that end there, to here. It wouldn't take nothin' to do."

Ned purposely bumped the door against the wall, and the two of them turned around. Shank took his hand off Abby and stepped toward Ned.

"Nice to see you again, Mr. Chapdelaigne," Shank said. "I was just showing your wife here how easy it would be to put in a ceiling fan. Cool you right down. Won't cost nothing compared to air-conditioning."

"Well, that's very nice of you to think of us."

Shank had his usual uniform on—ripped, grease-stained blue jeans, a plaid, flannel shirt with the sleeves cut off, and a painter's cap that had been speckled with every paint color imaginable. Ned was sure Shank saw the cap as a badge of honor, like the stickers World War II flying aces used to put on their planes commemorating each fighter they'd downed.

Shank pulled at his graying beard and looked up at the ceiling again. "I just wanted to come by and see your place," he said. "I almost always do that, you know—before we hold class. I like to scope out the situation so I come prepared, and I take a look around to see if there's anything else I can help you folks out with. I could give you a real good price on a ceiling fan, for example."

"Thank you, Mr. Shank," said Ned. "We'll keep that in mind."

Shank walked around the living room, looking up at the ceiling, knocking on the walls, and nodding his head as if he were giving his approval. At one point, he brushed up against Abby, who stumbled a little as she tried to back away from him. Shank grabbed her by the shoulders, saying, "Excuse me, excuse me. Steady now."

"Mr. Shank," Ned said, but Shank had gone off into the kitchen. Ned and Abby followed. He opened a couple of cabinets, swinging the doors on their hinges and running his hand across the grain of the wood. Then he looked up at the ceiling again and paced back and forth, dragging his feet with each step. He was making scuff marks on the linoleum floor with his boots. Ned was about to put a stop to it when Shank stood there with his hands on his hips, nodding again.

"Yep," he said, staring at Abby's chest, "this is a mighty fine piece of real estate you got here, Mr. Chapdelaigne. I certainly am envious."

"You haven't seen where we want to do the plastering yet," Ned said.

"Oh, don't you worry. I've got that covered. Plaster work is good for everyone to learn. I'm just glad someone needs it done so we can have a demonstration."

"Well, we're glad we could help," said Abby.

"Now, you just think about that ceiling fan in the living room. And if you want to reface these cabinets, we can do that, too. You just let me know."

Shank tracked his boots across the new floors and went out the front door, Abby following him. Ned grabbed a rag and scrubbed at the trail of scuff marks in the living room, cursing under his breath. Out on the porch, he heard Abby saying, "I've got lots of great food for us tomorrow. I'm looking forward to having everyone over."

"Oh, we're sure to have a grand time if you're entertaining us, Mrs. Chapdelaigne," said Shank. "I look forward to it, too."

Abby came back in all aglow as Shank's truck rumbled away. Her white sneakers pattered over the shiny floor. Ned didn't look up past her knees, but he could feel her energy. It annoyed him. Shank had sucked the spirit right out of him. A few minutes ago he was thinking about trying to make love to his wife for the first time in their new house; now, he didn't even have enough motivation to continue working on the doors.

"That man is an ingrate," he said to Abby as she returned from the kitchen with a glass of iced tea in her hand. "I loathe the idea of him coming back into our house."

"Lighten up, Ned," Abby said. "He's just an old man. His wife's dead. He's got nothing better to do."

"Well, if he's bored or lonely, why can't he join a senior center or something? Why does he have to come around and bother us on Saturday?

And I can't stand the way he looks at you. I think he's lecherous."

"Oh, I should be so lucky if you look at me that way when you're his age."

"Yeah, if I'm not dead," Ned said.

Abby traipsed off without a response, leaving him to finish scrubbing the floor on his hands and knees. He never thought about being Shank's age one day. The prospect of it almost seemed inconceivable. He didn't see himself growing old. He always imagined he'd be dead long before Abby. Not that he wanted to die or anything, but he knew he was difficult. Sometimes he thought his not being around would be a good thing for her. She could get on with her life, maybe even remarry and have less of a struggle. Do it right next time. At the same time, he couldn't picture her with anybody else without getting jealous. Even an old man like Shank threatened him. Before they'd bought the house, he'd been waiting for that one thing, that one final piece of weight that would make their relationship cave in. It didn't come, he surmised, because Abby's perseverance wouldn't allow it.

Abby went up to the loft, exasperated. She was finding it more and more difficult to engage Ned in any kind of meaningful conversation. More and more she found herself disengaging when conflict arose. They couldn't even fight well anymore. "The fighting is okay," the therapist had said, "as long as it's productive." If it wasn't going to be productive, she figured she might as well skip it.

She opened the windows in the loft to let some air in. It was warm and she looked forward to getting an air-conditioner so that she could sit in the studio without sweating on summer evenings. A breeze blew in, relieving the heat a bit, and Abby looked out at the house. It was an impressive structure, if she said so herself. She had no regrets; the price was a steal and with the money Ned's father bequeathed them they were able to afford it. It was so much better than the sterile condo they'd last rented. Now they had a small yard, four bedrooms, a basement, a garage—plenty of room to grow. She imagined children filling out the house eventually, but she did her best to keep that to herself.

She had pressured Ned enough throughout the history of their relationship. It seemed to go all the way back to when she vetoed the restaurant he had selected on their first date. He wanted Italian, but she wanted to try a new Middle Eastern place. Ned picked at his food and spread it around his plate; he sulked. She had no interest in going out with him again until weeks later when she saw another woman giggling on his arm at an event she was catering. During a moment when the other woman was in the bathroom, Abby told him she hoped he'd enjoy the food more than on their date and that she'd be happy to accommodate any special requests he might have. "Make it as bland as possible," he said and then he smiled coyly at her. He held one of her hands with both of his. "I hope I didn't sour you too much that time we went out. I'm sorry I was such a brat." He squeezed her hand firmly and she felt a warmth that she hadn't before. His hands were soft and light, and later that night all she could think about was how she wanted to touch them again. A man with hands like that, she thought, would never hurt her.

And truly he hadn't—at least not in an extreme sense. Their relationship had seesawed back and forth for years, with Abby always trying to push it ahead. She felt slightly guilty for pressing Ned on things he said he was not ready for. She had been the one to suggest they move in together. She had been the one to push for them to get married. But she felt if she didn't apply any pressure that he never would have moved forward, that he would still be living in his efficiency apartment in Manchester, seeing her only every Wednesday and Saturday night.

Now they at least had a house she would be proud of and he was finally on a tenure track. They had a chance to get settled. First things first, though. Refinish the floors, paint the downstairs, fix all the doors, paint the upstairs, work on the loft, plant a garden, prepare for children. All in due time, if she wasn't deluding herself, which she was sure was entirely possible.

*   *   *

Abby woke up on Sunday worrying about the food. Through the first three classes so far, standard procedure was to do the work first and eat afterward. But that was such a distraction, she thought. By the time they finished whatever project they were involved in, they were tired and probably dirty. It would be better to eat first while everyone was still fresh so they could get the most out of the food instead of just stuffing their faces to satisfy hunger. Then, after the plastering was done, they could relax and have drinks.

Of course, Ned would hear nothing of it. He went into a tirade, quoting his father about how one had to "earn his food." Labor, he said, builds up appetite, and "one of the great satisfactions derived from labor is often the meal awaiting at the other end of the job. Take that payment away and you take away incentive, you take away drive. Productivity goes down. The system collapses."

Abby had no desire to engage Ned in his defense of capitalism. He was baiting her, trying to start an argument, and she wouldn't give him the satisfaction.

"*Your* system has already collapsed," she said. "I don't see your productivity going up any time soon!" She stormed out of the house to water the gardenias she'd planted the other day, resolved that at the very least she would put out the crab dip and hummus so people could eat it as they arrived.

Ned went downstairs and began work on one of the battleship doors, thinking that the fights were slowly squelching his sex drive. He wondered how long they could live in the house without making love. He figured after a certain point it would go on indefinitely. Eventually they could even sleep in separate bedrooms. Maybe it'd be a good thing. Being able to stretch out might be better for his aching back. They'd grow to be an old, dried-up couple, until one of them died off and the other lived out loathsome days for the rest of his or her life.

He got angry at himself for thinking so much and not focusing on the task at hand. "The doors, you dummy," he said quietly to himself. "Focus on the doors." He scraped a battleship door until he could finally see the grain of the wood and his arms were tired and his hands had turned gray.

He didn't come upstairs until three couples had already arrived at the house. Abby had corralled them in the living room where they sat crunching vegetables and discussing the dip. "Mighty fine dip," someone was saying. "Is this real crab meat?" said someone else. "I'll have to get the recipe," said another. "Is this hummus? Delicious," Ned heard.

Abby sat there, a big celery stick in her hand, beaming, gloating even, Ned thought. For a second he tried to imagine her thirty years from now with the celery hanging out of her mouth. She would be old, worn, and tired, her skin sagging, her hair thinned and white. She would be bitter. It would be his fault.

Two more couples came in and he had a house full of people who he wished were not there, and it was about to get worse. Carl Shank arrived fashionably late, in uniform, with a sledgehammer in one hand and a bucket of plaster in the other. He put the plaster down, but carried the sledgehammer with him to the coffee table where he sunk a chip into the crab dip. A chunk of crab meat fell and hung in his beard for a second until he wiped it away with the back of his hand. Then he made a face as if he were in ecstasy and shook his head back and forth saying, "That there is the best crab dip I've had in years."

"Thank you, Carl," Abby said, and he nodded and winked at her.

"I have to say," said Shank, "it sure is a pleasure to be welcomed into the Chapdelaignes' new home. And what a beauty it is. It needs some work, but this is a fine piece of property, isn't it, folks?"

"Very nice, very nice," a couple of people said at the same time.

"And you wait 'til we get through with it," Shank said. "This place will really be worth something. I'm in the reconstruction business, and I see a lot we can do here. With a little bit of effort this is going to be one prime piece of real estate."

The rest of the group echoed his sentiments until someone suggested that Abby give them a tour of the house.

"Sure, sure," she said, pretending she was bashful about it, but in reality she had been hoping someone would ask.

The group followed her into the kitchen, Ned bringing up the rear, nervous because Shank still carried the sledgehammer with him. He rested it on a countertop but still held onto it while Abby apologized for the mess that had accumulated because they hadn't finished unpacking yet. Shank was determined to reface those cabinets, Ned thought, and this was his chance to gouge them so they would need to be redone. Ned watched him very closely, staring down at the hammer while he stood by Shank's side.

"But you must see my loft above the garage!" Abby said. "Ned said I could have it as a moving-in present. A place I can go to when I need to get away from him. I told him I'll be moving in there next week!"

Everyone snickered. Shank belted out a deep laugh, holding his belly with his free hand.

Abby herded them out of the kitchen and into the backyard, where she gestured elegantly toward the door above the garage, like Vanna White motioning to a new puzzle on *Wheel of Fortune*.

"We still haven't figured out how the old residents used that door," Abby said. "Doesn't it add character to the backyard?"

They all followed her up the stairs to the loft, Ned and Shank, still with the sledgehammer, the last two in line. Abby gave the door a shove and it squeaked like it was going to fall off its hinges as it opened. Ned looked back at the house. It was a big house, he noted—far bigger than two people needed. It rose above them, stretching up toward the top of an elm tree that was planted near the driveway. It was a big tree and Ned foresaw it doing all sorts of damage over the years, with its roots sprawling into the basement and its branches hovering over the roof. He saw himself perched on the roof one day with a hand saw, battling the tree as it stretched out over the telephone and cable lines. Raking leaves was one thing, cleaning gutters was another. The last thing he wanted was to be up on that roof. Just standing on the top of the garage stairs now made him feel like his vertigo was coming back. He held onto the handrail until he safely made it to the top.

Inside the loft, he was surprised at how much Abby had done to it already. She'd really cleaned it up. It was hot inside the studio, but the musty smell was gone. She'd painted the walls a glossy white that made the place much brighter and more inviting. A new coat of paint made the windowpanes look brand new. She'd laid down a carpet that was soft under Ned's feet. She'd even begun to bring some of his books up. His entire Roman Empire reference collection was arranged nicely on bookshelves in the far corner, next to a new, small desk and a chair. On the wall near the aberrant door, she'd hung his favorite map—a depiction of Napoleon's march to Moscow. It gave a solemn quality to the room, which Ned rather liked. Over 400,000 men invaded Russia in 1812. Only 10,000 of them returned. The French army was decimated by a harsh winter and tactical hubris. He could only imagine what the soldiers went through. And all he had to do was climb on the roof to clean the gutters.

He began to see that the loft had potential and he felt he'd been awfully idiotic when he disparaged Abby's idea of turning it into a studio. He didn't understand why he was the way he was. When things got tough, his first reaction was to flee instead of bunkering down and fighting for something worthwhile like his wife did. Abby was a soldier all right. She would have survived the march to and from Moscow. He couldn't say the same for himself. It had always been that way in their relationship. He'd nearly left her several times, feeling there was an ever-widening gap between them. He never felt like he was capable of tossing a rope to the other side and trying to cross the divide. It was too strenuous.

The class participants lavished praise on Abby for the work she'd done on the loft. She looked to Ned for a sign of his approval and he managed a smile and a wink.

"This is going to be a fine place once you're done with it," someone said.

"It's a marvelous work in progress," said another.

"Keep going," said someone else. "All it takes is a little hard work."

She beamed with satisfaction, as if this gave validation to her plan for a home and a future. It was ridiculous, she thought, that she needed a bunch of people she barely knew to give her some kind of affirmation. She needed to get that from Ned, but adoration was never his strong suit.

"I'm pleased you all like it," she said. "It's definitely going to be my pet project." She went on to say how much she wanted to do to the house before she started to look for catering work in the area. "This is definitely just the beginning," she said.

Shank had been quiet during all of this, Ned noticed. He looked the studio over carefully, checking out the ceiling—for a ceiling-fan job, no doubt—and tapping his finger against the walls as he walked from one end of the room to the other. Ned eyed him suspiciously. He was on the far end of the loft, near the map of Napoleon's march, when Abby suggested they head back. She'd become so elated that she didn't even mind doing the plastering first and serving her main course afterward.

"Well," she said, "I know we have a lot of work to do, so why don't we go back to the house and get started."

"Well, why don't we get started right here?" Shank said. Ned, who had been stepping toward the door, turned around just in time to see the old man grip the sledgehammer with both hands and heave it at the wall.

"Right here's just fine," Shank said, bits of plasterboard flying across the room. The sight of it immobilized Ned for a second, as if he had just slipped into an alternate reality and couldn't comprehend what everybody was yelling about. He snapped out of it by the time Shank punched a second hole underneath Napoleon's march. The framed map fell from its mount and landed on the carpet, which was now covered with pieces of the wall.

"A plaster job is the easiest thing in the world to do," Shank said. "We can get this back to normal in no time."

Ned was finally moving by the time Shank raised the hammer again. He popped it into the wall for a third time, right by the red door, before Ned got to him and ripped it out of his hands. The hammer thumped to the floor and Ned shoved Shank into the wall.

"What are you doing?" he screamed at him. "We need plastering in our bedroom!"

"Well, I'll show you how to do it here and you can plaster wherever you want later," Shank said. "And don't be pushing me, Mr. Chapdelaigne." Shank pointed his finger into Ned's chest. Ned slapped it away and bumped up against him. He couldn't believe he was doing this. Had he lost his mind?

They grabbed each other by the shirts and tussled awkwardly like a couple of walruses. Ned could hear Abby screaming, "Stop it, stop it!" But he couldn't let go. The two men jockeyed back and forth, their shoes crunching the plasterboard beneath them. Ned could hear the agitated voices of his guests all around him. It sounded like he was in the middle of a school-yard fight. He thought it was never going to end until Shank spun him around and flung him into the red door. He crashed into it face first. The lock snapped and the door shot open, careening out over the yard on its hinges. Ned felt his feet drop out from underneath him and grabbed the doorknob. He swung out over the yard, the hinges creaking painfully under his weight.

He held on tight to both ends of the knob, but the door hung out there, far enough away from the loft so that nobody could reach him. He saw Shank holding his hand out toward him, but Ned yelled at the old man to keep away from him. At least, he thought he yelled at him. He wasn't sure. The hinges squeaked loudly each time he shifted his weight. Everyone was shouting various things at him. He wished they'd stop. All the screaming was breaking his concentration.

He reasserted his grip and wondered if this was how his father could hold a frozen muffler pipe in his bare hand in the dead of winter— because he had to. He wondered what made one man persevere and survive the long, frozen march back from Moscow and what made another die in his tracks right there on the trail. He wondered if there was any small part of him that had what it'd take to be one of the 10,000 survivors that crossed the Berezina and eventually made it back over the Polish border. He imagined Napoleon would have seen him as unfit for enlistment. "You won't even make it to Poland," he imagined the general saying. "You're not going to make a difference. Stay in France. Stay alive."

How humiliating. He couldn't even have been conscripted by a nineteenth-century dictator.

"But I just shoved an old man with a sledgehammer against a wall. There was considerable peril there. That must be good for something?"

"If you're not shot along the way, you'll likely freeze to death, and if you don't freeze to death, you'll probably drown crossing a river."

"Still, I can't just stay here in France forever. I'm stagnating. I'm going to have to leave sooner or later. Send me to Moscow! I can make it—I think."

"Very well then. Choose your weapon, son. You have a long road ahead of you. Personally, I don't think you'll survive, but I'm not one to snuff out the spirit of any man. Take your weapon and be gone with you! All you can do is your paltry best."

Ned wondered if his paltry best would be good enough to save his marriage—if it was good enough to have children and climb up onto the roof when he needed to. There was no way of knowing. Abby was reaching for him, holding her hand out, down on her knees in the big, open space in the wall where the door used to be. "Come on, honey, you can do it," she was saying. "Just swing your weight over to the left."

He wanted to tell her to hang on a second. He wasn't quite ready to come down yet. He was on a white horse, galloping off somewhere, following one of Napoleon's lieutenants. The wind was whipping through his hair and the autumn breeze felt good. He didn't know what winter would bring, but he'd cross that bridge when he came to it.

Just a few more minutes, he wanted to tell Abby. He'd be there for her in just a few more minutes. He had a lot of thoughts flying through his mind at the moment, but he was reaching a plateau, and he'd be able to come down soon.

About the Author

Bob Bobala's writing has appeared in *Newsweek, The Washington Post, North Dakota Quarterly, The Portland Review, Innisfree, Spectrum,* online at The Motley Fool, and in other newspapers and journals. He taught fiction writing at the University of Maryland-College Park, where he received an MFA in creative writing, and as a returning faculty member for the Johns Hopkins Center for Talented Youth (CTY) summer programs. He grew up in Chicopee, Massachusetts and attended the University of Massachusetts at Amherst. Currently, he lives in La Jolla, California.

www.ingramcontent.com/pod-product-compliance
Lightning Source LLC
Chambersburg PA
CBHW051841170626
46807CB00003B/1286